C. Fell Smith

Stephen Crisp and his Correspondents

1657-1692

C. Fell Smith

Stephen Crisp and his Correspondents
1657-1692

ISBN/EAN: 9783337109189

Printed in Europe, USA, Canada, Australia, Japan

Cover: Foto ©Raphael Reischuk / pixelio.de

More available books at **www.hansebooks.com**

STEVEN CRISP

AND HIS

CORRESPONDENTS,

1657-1692,

BEING A SYNOPSIS OF THE LETTERS IN THE

"COLCHESTER COLLECTION,"

EDITED, WITH NOTES AND AN INTRODUCTION,

BY C. FELL SMITH.

London :

E. Hicks, Jun., 14, Bishopsgate Without, and 2, Amen Corner,
Paternoster Row.

1892,

PREFACE.

ABOUT two years ago, while preparing the article on John Kendall for *The Dictionary of National Biography*, I first learned of the existence of the MSS. herein summarized. I at once became anxious that documents of such genuine and historical interest should be rendered more accessible, they being then in a somewhat torn and damp condition. They have now, through the prompt generosity of Mr. Wilson Marriage, Mayor of Colchester, been cleaned, mended, and bound in a handsome folio volume, under the supervision of Mr. F. B. Bickley, of the MSS. Department of the British Museum. To both of these my thanks are due. Mr. Marriage's knowledge of the history of Colchester has also been of much assistance to me.

The future student of early quaker history will now be able to refer to the manuscripts, upon application to the Clerk of the Monthly Meeting of Colchester. To this body of Friends I tender thanks for permission to study them at length ; to Mr. J. J. Beuzemacher, B.A. B. Mus., for some assistance with the Dutch MSS., and to my cousin, Mr. Miller Christy, F.L.S., for many valuable suggestions while seeing the work through the press.

With regard to the word "Quaker," which I have frequently used, I trust it will offend no one. In contemporary literature outside the Society, it is the only one used, and, although originally bestowed in jest, it, and the body bearing it, have long since taken up a position honoured by all classes of society.

Some small portions of the present work have appeared in *The British Friend*, and I here thank the editor, Mr. J. G. Smeal, for permission to republish them.

C. FELL SMITH.

Gt. Saling, Essex,
    May, 1892.

TABLE OF CONTENTS.

	PAGE
PREFACE	v.
INTRODUCTION	ix.
SYNOPSIS OF LETTERS IN THE COLCHESTER COLLECTION	1
DISTRAINTS AND IMPRISONMENTS IN ESSEX, 1656-1670	67
APPENDIX A—WILL OF STEVEN CRISP	76
„ B—THE CRISP PAPERS AT DEVONSHIRE HOUSE	78
INDEX	80

LIST OF ILLUSTRATIONS.

COLCHESTER CASTLE. *From a photograph.* . - - Frontispiece

STEBBING MEETING HOUSE. *Drawn by E. Cupper.* - To face p. xvi.

FACSIMILE OF CRISP'S ANSWERS TO THE DEPUTY
LIEUTENANTS - - - - - - - „ xxiv.

DOORWAY OF THE PRISON IN COLCHESTER CASTLE. *From
a drawing by Ernest Poppy* - - - - „ xl.

GEORGE FOX. *From a Phototype of the painting by Sir
Peter Lely, at Swarthmoor College, Philadelphia* ., liv.

PORTRAIT OF THE PRINCESS ELIZABETH. *From a Print
at Devonshire House* - - - - - „ 20

PORTRAIT OF JAMES NAYLER. *Painted and engraved
by Francis Place* - - - - - „ 48

AN AMSTERDAM QUAKER - - - - - - 65

COTTAGE AT SALING, FORMERLY A MEETING HOUSE
Drawn by E. Capper - - - - „ 70

INTRODUCTION.

The Collection of MSS. now edited were bequeathed by Steven Crisp, of Colchester, to the Monthly Meeting of that place, and after his death, in 1692, they remained obscure and unheeded for more than a century. John Kendall, of Colchester, the quaker philanthropist, and a scholar of no mean ability, made a small selection from them in his " Letters of I. Penington, to which are added Letters of Steven Crisp, William Penn, R. Barclay, and others" (Lond., 1796), and it was proposed by the editors of " Collectitiæ" (York, 1824), to include the most important of the remainder. This publication, however, proceeded only to the fourth number, and although parts or the whole of twenty-two letters were given in the two volumes, both are now so seldom seen that they are practically useless for any purposes of reference.

In this end of the nineteenth century—undoubtedly a time of publishing—from some cause or another, perhaps from the spread of individual thought and inquiry, awakened by vast strides of scientific knowledge which cannot be ignored, a large amount of curiosity has been manifested in the early rising and doings of that most individual of all the sects, the Quakers.

Springing, as they did, from the spiritual enthusiasm of an enquiring, but untutored, Leicestershire shoemaker, and assuming in the space of less than fifty years the vast proportions of 100,000 members, they formed a power in the nation whose influence has been surely felt. From the very first, the position they occupied was singular. Their hand was against every man, and every man's hand against them. Churchmen, Papists, Anabaptists, Seekers, Ranters, Familists, Presbyterians, no matter what a man's creed, he was mistaken in theory and wrong in practice to the quaker who had imbibed the teaching of the "inward Light." And, in their dogged adherence to their own convictions, their resolute performance of duties they conceived imposed on them by conscience, in the face of insult and molestation, they undoubtedly set on foot the scheme of toleration which every day is rendering more and more perfect.

The greatest number of recruits for the new Society were, of course, humble unlettered persons, but there also joined the ranks (beside Penn and Barclay, whose names are synonymous with early Quakerism) men like Samuel Fisher, Thomas Lawson, and Richard Claridge, all of whom received university training, and took orders in the Church of England before turning quakers.

Steven Crisp did not belong to either the humble or the more highly educated. He was a typical example of the middle class, well educated (for he could write in fair Latin) diligent in business, and owning a competency sufficient to free him for those continued travels for the spreading of his new principles, in which his after life was spent. His was a life of considerable importance to the student of early quaker history, for from his personal and intellectual gifts, as a man of extreme judgment and amiability, as well as of considerable culture and large views, the position he held was that of a central pillar in the edifice of the new church which was in the process of being reared. His residence, moreover, in his native town of Colchester, and his acquaintance with the Dutch language, peculiarly fitted him to be the connecting link between the large body of converts in Holland, and the pioneers of quakerism in England. From Harwich, all those who visited the towns of Amsterdam, The Hague, Embden, Quedlinburg, Groningen, and others where the new faith had penetrated, set sail ; and Steven Crisp's house in Moor Lane became the resort, in going and returning, of many earnest men and women, by whose exertions the spread of quakerism was secured. It was in this way, as well as by his constant travels in all parts of England, Scotland, Holland, and Germany, that Steven Crisp made such a large circle of acquaintances.

The present volume notices letters to or from no less than fifty-two different persons. Among his correspondents will be found the Princess Elizabeth of the Palatine, eldest daughter of the unfortunate Queen of Bohemia, and grand daughter of James I., the pupil of Descartes, and one of the most talented women of her time. Crisp had intended to visit her, but he was prevented by illness and the length of the journey. He therefore wrote her an *Epistle*, printed in his "Works," p. 406. To this probably her letter, No. 22, is the reply, the date of it being about 1672. Benjamin Furly, the friend of Algernon Sidney and John Locke; John Rous, the son of a wealthy West Indian planter, who married Margaret Fell; James Parnel, the first Quaker who paid for his principles with his life, and under whose preaching Crisp first heard of quakerism; William Caton, who afterwards became his brother-in-law; Mrs. Judith Zinspenning Sewel, the mother of the quaker historian, and a woman of singular talent, together with many other persons, equally well known and historically interesting, are to be met and conversed with in these letters, written in the quaint, crabbed handwriting of the seventeenth century. Of Sewel himself, we have a glimpse in a letter from Wm. Caton, when he was twelve years old, "He lives with his uncle, learns Latin, and is very apt at study, but childish in other things."

The character of Crisp is very finely developed in the course of this correspondence, and he is seen holding an almost unique position in the Society, to which his robust, uncompromising directness, tempered by extreme justice, judgment, tact, and something more of the spirit of conciliation than distinguished some of its earliest members, made him invaluable. Thus he became the arbitrator in disputes, the adviser in matters legal and political of the Society, and the stern and wise rebuker of the foolish, fanatical, or contumacious.

In all these lights do the letters reveal him, busy ever, as he says in his autobiography, " helping and assisting the Lords people according to my ability, both in their spiritual and temporal concerns, as the Lord of my life gave me an understanding . . . for he opened me in many things relating to the affairs of this world that I might be as a staff to the weak in those things, and might stand by the widow and fatherless and plead the right of the poor, in all which I sought neither honour nor profit, and He whom I feared was my reward." As Josiah Coale, Crisp's companion on one of the journeys to Holland, rather lamely, but well-meaningly, expresses it, in his letter from Guilford, 12th Nov., 1661 (No. 107), his " share both in sufferings and re-joicings, has been as large as any, and in some sense more large ; for many although they are upright, have not the sense to feel the weights and burthens which many ways may be occasioned, as some others have, who must bear the burthen of the weak that they may be eased ; and some-times must bear the burthens of the wicked also, and of false brethren, which is the greatest suffering of all ; and this I know thou art not insensible of, but hast had thy share."

The letter (No. 24) addressed to William Penn by Crisp, in 1684, gives us an insight into the position he ultimately attained, when he could write in such a strain to a man of eminence and scholarship so widely acknowledged as the Founder of Pennsylvania. A small portion of the letter is here given.

" Dear William, I have had a great exercise of spirit concerning thee, which none knows . . . For my spirit hath been much bowed into thy concern and difficulty of thy present circumstance ; and I have had a sense of the various spirits, and intricate cares, and multiplicity affairs, and they of various kinds, which daily attend thee, and are enough to drink up thy spirit and tire thy soul, and which, if it is not kept to inexhaustible fountain, may be dried up. And this I must tell thee which thou also knowest, that the highest capacity of natural wit and parts, will not and cannot perform what thou hast to do, viz., to propagate and advance the interest and profit of the government and plantation [Pennsylvania] . . . There is a wisdom in government that hath respect to its own preservation, by setting up what is profitable to it, and suppressing what may be a detriment ; and this is the image of the true wisdom . . . There is a power on earth, by which princes declare justice, this is the image ; and there is a power which is heavenly . . and this is the substance . . . He that is a true delegate in this power can do great things for Gods glory, and shall have his reward, and shall be a judge of the tribes.

I hope thou will bear this my style of writing to thee. My spirit is under great weight at the writing thereof, and much I have in my heart, because I love thee well . . . My prayer to God is for thee, and you all, that you may be kept in the Lord's pure and holy way ; and above all for thee dear W. P., whose feet are upon a mountain, by which the eyes of many are upon thee ; the Lord furnish thee with wisdom, courage, and a sound judgment, prefer the Lord's interest, and he will make thy way prosperous."

In Penn's reply, he writes rather playfully of a letter from Gertrude Dericks, enclosed in Crisp's, in which she questions him about some cannon of anti-quaker proclivities. "There was an old timber house," he says, "below a gaol, above the sessions house, that had seven small, old iron cannon upon the green about it, some on the ground, others on broken carriages ; not one soldier, or arms borne, or militia-man seen, since I was first in Pennsylvania. So that I am as innocent of any act of hostility as she herself ; for the guns lying so, without soldiers, powder, bullet, or any garrison, is no more than if she bought a house with a musket in it ; and the guns are to go to New York, for they belong to that place ; however, I take it kindly of her."

Steven Crisp was born in Colchester, in August of the year 1628. He was the son of Steven and Elizabeth Crisp, who both joined the Society about the same time as their son. Previous to 1655, there is no information to hand about the Crisp family. They probably lived in Colchester, although

we find a widow and three children of that name, living at
St. Osyth.   Steven, senior, took an active part in the local
affairs of Friends, and his name appears on various appointments in the Meeting Book of the time.   He is always spoken
of in affectionate terms by his son, and he and his wife are
mentioned by Judith Zinspenning, in her letter to Crisp in
1664 (No. 33).   Within a year of that time, Elizabeth Crisp,
Steven's mother, died of the plague, which carried off so
many in Colchester.   She was buried in Moor Lane.   His
father lived until the 24th of January, 1672, when he died,
aged about fifty-six, and was buried in the "New
Yard."

The final entry in the present Collection, singularly enough,
alludes to him as follows :—"Distrained upon acct: of the
Late Act against Meetings wch took place ye 10th of 3rd mo.,
1670.   By warrant from the Mayor, Recorder, and Justices
of the town. . .   Steven Crisp, senior, fined 5s., had taken
from him two blankets, valued at 10s."

The younger Steven seems to have been a remarkably serious
child, and with a conscience abnormally developed.   In his
autobiography he says :—"When I was about nine or ten years
old, I sought the power of God with great diligence and earnest-
ness, with strong cries and tears ; and if I had had the whole
world, I would have given it, to have known how to obtain
the power over my corruptions.   And when I saw the care-
lessness of other children, and their profaneness, and that
they did not, that I could discern, think of God, nor were in
trouble, though they were far more wicked than I in their
speech and actions—Ah, Lord ! thought I, what will become
of these, seeing so heavy a hand is upon me, I can find
neither peace nor assurance of Thy love ?"   Then he goes on
to relate how his "ears were lent to the discourses and dis-
putations of the times, which were very many ; and one
while I let in one thing, and another while another," so he
"grew a very persevering hearer and regarder of the best
ministers, as they were reputed, and went with as much

diligence and cheerfulness to reading and to hearing sermons, as other children went to their play and sportings."

In this simple remark, we can trace some analogy to the contradictions of the times, which, while frivolous and licentious on the one hand, were, on the other, so imbued with the stern spirit of an austere religion, that even the tender child of twelve was drawn into the contemplation of the mysteries of the doctrine of election. He describes his sufferings in lurid colours. " In this iron furnace I toiled and laboured, and none knew my sorrows and griefs, which, at times, were almost intolerable, that I wished I had never been born, or that my end might be like the beasts of the field; for I counted them happy, since they had no such bitter conflict here as I had, nor should endure that hereafter, which I feared I must endure after all."

It may have been the recollection of these childish torments that prompted him, many years after, to bring out " A New Book for Children to learn in, or the Child's Primer," 1681. Whether from the influence of his collaborator or no, the little book, written in conjunction with George Fox the younger, abounds in stern invective and somewhat involved theology, little suited to children, but it became apparently much used by Dutch and English parents.

When he was about seventeen, Crisp began attending the meetings of the Separatists in Colchester, and continued more or less attached to that body for some time. What part he played in the stirring events that followed 1641, we cannot say. Doubtless he remained in Colchester during the siege, sharing with the other inhabitants, the privations of famine and distress, endured in common with the Royalist garrison, with whom they were so little in sympathy. Colchester, as a town, was, from the first dawn of the conflict, of strong Puritan and Parliamentarian sympathies.

Crisp was probably entirely occupied with his business, which was that of bays or baize-making. The material was a coarse kind of flannel, very much shrunk, and former-

ly more in use than at the present time. Its manufacture
was a substantial industry in Essex, having been introduced
by the Flemings about 1570 (Morant, vol. i. p. 75). It was
extensively carried on at Halstead and Bocking, but Colchester was the principal centre. Cromwell in his " History
of Colchester " (London, 1825, p. 288) says:—" It has even been
calculated that the trade brought the town a return of
£30,000 weekly." All " bays " were searched and sealed in
the Dutch Bay Hall, at Colchester, and the fines for fraudu-
lent measurements and materials were distributed with
great exactitude to the poor, in cloth. The fines from
the English merchants were given to the English poor, and
those from the Dutch merchants to the Dutch poor. The
greatest amount thus collected in any year, was £243 5s. 3d.
in 1683, which was about the time of the Bay and Say
makers' highest prosperity. It will be seen by a reference to
p. 74 that " bay lists " were taken from the Friends for
fines, &c. The Dutch congregation was allowed the use of one
of the parish churches, until they acquired one of their own,
Wright (" History of Essex," vol. i., p. 335) says in Head-street,
with a house for the minister. The wooden frame-work of
this was sent ready to put together from Holland. Wright
gives a description of the house, which was burned down
early in this century, and says a window frame in the front
bore the date 1677. Morant gives the situation of the Dutch
church as St. Mary's Lane. Wherever it was, the congregation
was dissolved in 1728, their trade having been ruined by the
wars with Spain. There are a few interesting notes on the
successive ministers of this church, in Burn's " History of
Foreign Protestant Refugees " (Lond. 1846, p. 214).

Steven Crisp married in the year 1648, when he was twenty
years old. His marriage register has, so far, not been traced.
His wife's name was Dorothy. She joined the Society with
her husband, and was in high esteem among the Friends, for
in the early Women's Meeting book still preserved at Colchester, her name occurs with much regularity, on various

Stebbing Meeting House, built 1675.

F. Capper

appointments up to the time of her death. She is occasionally mentioned in these and other letters. In one from Crisp, dated Amsterdam, 20th April, 1663, addressed probably to John Furly, of Colchester, he says :—"Tell my dear Dorothy that I intend next post to write to her ; or by Feedham, if he come." (Kendall's Letters, p. 101.) Soon after his marriage, Steven Crisp settled in the house where the remainder of his life in Colchester was spent. It was in the old Moor, or Moor Elms Lane, now Priory St., which ran along the outside of the town wall from below East Gate, and passing the south-eastern corner of the wall, fell in St. Botolph St. It was named from the "more" or garden belonging to St. Botolph's Priory, which adjoined the lane.

Steven and Dorothy Crisp had two children, both of whom died young. A daughter, named after Steven's mother, Elizabeth, died during the visitation of plague at Colchester, 1665 and 6. Between May 1665, and Oct. 1666, no less than ninety-eight Friends were buried, which affords a good idea of their numbers in Colchester at the time.

In June, 1655, Crisp heard of the arrival in the town of James Parnel. His fame had preceded him as a youth "filled with the name and power of the most High, and who had turned many to righteousness." Steven went to see him, and entered into argument, thinking, as he describes in his autobiography, by his superior years and experience, to easily withstand this young lad of eighteen. He himself was then twenty-seven. He "quickly came to perceive that the spirit of sound judgment was in Parnel, and the witness in himself," he adds, signified that he must "own it as being just and true." So the same day he went to a meeting and heard Parnel preach, and soon became a zealous quaker. Within two years, he was imprisoned in the Moot Hall at Colchester, "by the said William Motte, deputy recorder, for speaking to a priest in the same steeplehouse [St. Peter's], and then by the

B

Mayor and Aldermen set at liberty. And after that, he was indited again for the same, and fined twenty shillings by the sessions, and committed to prison again by John Vicars, Mayor in ye year 1657, till it should be paid, where he was kept some time." This authentic information about Crisp's earliest imprisonment, is to be found on fol. 297 of the Crisp Collection of MSS., " Imprisonments and Distraints in Essex."

From this visit of Parnel, dates the commencement of the Society in Essex. Friends shortly afterwards became numerous in every part of the county. Colchester became, and long remained the principal centre, owing largely to the receptivity of the Dutch population to imbibe the teaching of Fox. The first meetings in Colchester were probably held in private houses. As early as 1669 a burial ground in Moor Lane was presented by Thomas Bayles, and in 1672, a large Meeting House in St. Martin's Lane was purchased (see No. 108). In 1683 the building known as St. Helen's Chapel was purchased in addition, and both were used until about 1801, when another meeting-house was provided in East Stockwell Street. By 1667, the numbers of Friends had assumed such proportions in Essex, that, at a General Meeting held at Felstead, 13th of Sept., 1667, by George Fox's appointment, it was decided to divide the county into six Monthly Meetings, viz. :—Colchester, Coggeshall, Felstead, Ham and Waltham, Witham, and Thaxted. This arrangement remains still in force, although the nomenclature seems anomalous, since there are at present no Friends left at Felstead, Thaxted, or Witham, and for convenience sake, those meetings adjoining London, have been added to that Quarterly Meeting.

As the Society increased, Meeting Houses and burial grounds were built or purchased in many places. Some of the former, as Witham, Thaxted, and Felstead, have been long in disuse, or are let to other denominations. Friends from the first were careful to provide burial grounds near or adjoining all their Meeting Houses. George Fox set forth in No. XVI of his

"Friends Fellowship," 1668, reprinted as "Canons and Institutions," 1669, that "Friends do buy convenient burying-places, as Abraham did, who bought a place to bury his dead, . . . and let them be decently and well fenced." In the succeeding Canon, it is desired that Friends buy convenient books for registering the Births, Marriages, and Burials, and thus, in 1668, was instituted that admirable system which the Society has ever since practised.

The first Meeting House erected in Essex, is that still standing in the long, straggling village street of Stebbing, three miles from Dunmow. An illustration of this faces p. xvi. The date, 1675, and some ornamental scroll work over the door, are so reduced in the illustration that the former can scarcely be deciphered. The building is of thin red bricks, with an exceedingly conical roof. The casement windows and arched doorway at the side, are the oldest parts. A massive oaken bar fastens this door on the inside, the walls are panelled to about the height of these windows. The porch and windows in the front of the building are manifestly of later date. The ground on which this Meeting House stands, with, probably, a house or building afterwards converted or demolished, was, it appears from a MS. book at Colchester, purchased in 1675, of John Lane of Stebbing, for the sum of £30, by Thomas Child. In the same year, it was conveyed to five Friends, viz.: John Jesper, Stephen Chopping, Joseph Levitt, Francis Marriage, and William Evener. This list is interesting, for any person acquainted with Stebbing, will recognise at least four of these surnames as being, until recently, represented in the village.

In the same year, a Meeting House was purchased in the adjoining parish of Saling. The property consisted of a messuage or tenement, with garden, and a croft of about one acre. It was bought for the sum of £20, of William Crow, sen., and William Crow, jun., by Edward Mansfield, John Emson, John Peachy, John Smith, and John Start. The Crows

were evidently Friends, and appear to have been a family of
some note in the parish, for the road on which the cottage,
figured in our illustration facing p. 70, stands, is to this day
known as Crow's Green. The yew-tree I believe to have
been planted at this time. In the same year as it was purchased (1675), this property was, by the five Friends named,
conveyed to William Crow, his son William, John Mansfield,
Henry Smith, and Joseph Forster. In 1702, a fresh convey-
ance was made to Zachary Child, some of whose family were
among the earliest Friends imprisoned in Colchester Castle.
Zachary lived at Felstead, a village adjoining Stebbing.
Here also there was a meeting-house as we have seen, as early
as 1672. It was probably not the building now standing.

After this slight review of affairs in the county, we will
return to Crisp and his history. Notwithstanding all there
was to keep him in .Colchester, he, in 1659, was one of the
600 Friends who offered to "lie body for body" instead of
those who were then suffering in dungeons. These sub-
stitutes were not accepted.

It is not easy at the present time to understand the fear
and dread with which Crisp, and many other of the early
Friends, received the first intimations of their "call" to become travelling preachers for the truth. It meant, of course,
absence from home for frequent and prolonged intervals,
with but scanty and insufficient news from those they left ;
but they were only too well aware also, that it meant always
contempt and derision from the religious, as well as the pleasure-loving section of the people, and very often, direst
hardships, imprisonment, and even death.

. Crisp says he was loath to forsake his dear wife and children, his father and mother, and he would have pleaded his
own inability, the care of his family, his service in the meeting at Colchester, and many other things, that he might be
excused this thing that he had not looked for, but he found it
of no avail, so he gave up with "pretty much cheerfulness,"

and started some time in September, 1659, through Lincoln-shire and Yorkshire to Scotland, "to bear witness to that high professing nation."

Halting at York on the way north, he was roughly handled by the Mayor, who entered the meeting while Steven Crisp was at prayer, and dragged him violently into the street. In Scotland, too, he was sometimes ill received by the people, especially at Dalkeith, where, he says, "had not the soldiers appeared as a stop to their murderous purposes against me, their works of mischief had more appeared." He continues in his Journal, "I travelled to and fro that winter on foot, with cheerfulness. Many straits and difficulties attended me (which I forbear to mention), it being the time of the motion of the English and Scottish armies, upon which came the revolution of government, and the bringing back King Charles the Second into England."

During this northern journey, Crisp records that he "lacked nothing," yet all along a "secret hope" did live in him, that when it was safely accomplished, he should be freed from future service, and at liberty to return to his calling and family. In this hope, however, he was much mistaken, since his life from this time was but a long series of missionary visits to the colonies of quakers in all parts of England, and the north of Europe.

About January, 1660, Crisp turned his face homewards, and travelling through Westmoreland, Lancashire, and other coun-ties, he arrived at Cambridge in the end of June. On the 2nd of July, he assembled with the Friends there, "in their own hired house as usual," when a tumult of students, accompanied, it is said, by some of the senior Fellows and Proctors, with townsmen and boys, broke in upon them, spending their ill-advised fury in such ways, that they richly earned the des-cription given of them by Fox ("Journal," ed. 1765, p. 144), that "the miners, colliers, and carters could never be ruder." A letter dated 16th July, 1660, and signed by twenty-nine Friends (Besse's "Sufferings," vol. i., p. 88), describing the fury of the mob, who battered down large portions of the walls, was drawn up and presented by Margaret Fell to the King (see the endorsement of the MS. copy among the Crisp Papers at Devonshire House, App. B.); but the sole result was that an order was given in Council for the pulling down of the house. The same year, 120 Friends were imprisoned in Cambridge for refusing the oath of allegiance.

In his Journal, Crisp is uniformly silent about all his imprisonments. Perhaps he judged it sufficient that they were recorded in the official "Book of Sufferings," kept by each meeting by order of Fox. Among the queries annually made at that time, were the significant ones, " How many prisoners have you ? " and " How many have died prisoners ? " It is quite in keeping with Crisp's generous spirit, that in the whole of his diary, he only once vaguely mentions that " a prison became my portion, nigh two hundred miles from home." This happened in the same year, 1660. For when he had only been at home a few days, he " departed northward again at the commandment of the Lord." On the 11th of November, he was present at a meeting in the house of Simon Townsend, at Norton, in Durham. A party of soldiers, commanded by Captain Bellasis, came and arrested several present. They were carried before a justice, who commanded them to appear before the next sessions, which they did, and were at once committed to prison for refusing the oath of allegiance. Crisp was separately confined from the others, in company with one Thomas Turner. A letter written by them to the Deputy Lieutenants, &c., while in prison, is here printed, from the copy in Crisp's writing, preserved in the small bundle of Crisp papers at Devonshire House. It is endorsed *A coppy of our Remonstrance to the Deputy Lts. and Justices of Comitatis Durham.*

From the same source we have his answers to the Deputy Lieutenants, see facsimile p. xxiv., which is interesting, as it affords the earliest autobiographical information of Crisp. (For a transcript of this see p. liv.)

To the Deputy Lieutenants and ye Justices of Peace for ye County of Durham, or any of ym to whose hands this may come :—

"Ffriends, we having taken into serious consideration your civill demeanour towards us yesterday, which wee gratefully acknowledge (and thank ye Lord for it) and your moderation and soft flexable [nes] and temperatenes of spirit soe much appeared concerning us, in giving and allowing us liberty to speake for ourselves and for ye truth soe freely before you, and this we say is in you honorable and of good report, for indeed it soe becomes not only you but all ym yt are in authority : and this you will find tending to ye peace and tranquillity of these nations : as you are guided in moderation and in ye spirit of meekness, for ye fruit of this spirit is love, long-suffering, mercy, and forbearance, and who or what majestrate is found herein is blameless before ye Lord, and beares not ye sword in vaine. We therefore proceed to let you know and see how willing we are to comply with what may conduce to ye peace of the nation, and as neere as we can condescend to your requirings, still eyming [aiming] and minding to keepe ourselves in obedience to ye doctrine of Christ, which whosoever departs from, falls into condemnation : and thus to show you a testimony of our fidellity, and to retaliate your before-mentioned civility, we having well considered ye whole matter, doe thereupon declare as followeth :

That for ye removing of all jealousys and suspicions that hath or may arise in you, or any of you, concerning us your prisoners allegiance and subjection to ye king and his government over these nations, we doe solemnly and from our hearts declare in ye presence of him yt searcheth ye same, that we doe owne King Charles ye Second to bee lawfull king of these nations, and supream majestrate over ye same, with all ye territorys thereunto belonging. And that ye power of government, which God by a special power hath put into his hand, is not subordinate to any power, prince, potentate, emperor, king, man or men, counsel or counsels, in any nation under heaven. Neither doe wee believe, but utterly detest, that any power or just-right is in ye pope or see of Roome to depose him from this his dignity and government, or to dispose of any of ye lands and territorys unto which it extends, unto ye government and rule of any other pson or psons whatsoever, or to discharge us or any of his people in this nation, from their obedience and subjection to ye king, upon any pretence whatsoever. And further, wee doe pfesse and solemnly declare that we will neyther plot, nor conspire, nor contrive, any thing or matter against his pson or government, nor abett, assist, or hold confederacy with any that soe shall doe, but one ye contrary, shall as good subiects, both to him, and his successors, seeke to suppresse ye same what in us lyeth, and also to give ye truest and timelyest notice wee can of any such plott, contrivance, or conspiracy, to the king or sume of his faithfull officers and ministers, y^t they may suppresse ye same with most expedition. And farther wee doe declare in ye singlnes of our hearts, that our refusing any part of ye forme of words comonly used in this behalfe, is not from any reserved intention of disobedience, or to have unto ourselves a liberty of disloyalty, but only for conscience sake, upon consideration of some words in ye Holy Scriptures, and also wee doe hereby declare y^t if ever wee bee found acting any thing or things contrary to this our declaration and recognition, or anything thereunto [belonging, paper torn], then we say wee doe and shall acknowledge ourselves liable to such paines and penalties as are provided against those who having sworne allegiance to ye King, are found violating ye same, and to this our free and voluntary Ingagem^t we have cordially subscribed our names, and if it be required of us for confirmation of ye same, are also ready to sett to our seales.

S. C.   T. T.

At ye place of our confinement,
this 18 of ye ii °Mo. 1660."

In Vol. xxxi. of the State Papers (Domestic), at the Record Office, is a letter from Dr. John Barwick† to John Nicholas, dated Feb. 1661, in which he says that he "sends some intercepted letters and papers, by which it is clear that the leaders of the Quakers stand on punctilios of honour. He has had conferences at the sessions, at the request of the justices, with Crisp, of Colchester, the leader of them in the county, who had given hopes of relenting, but his only answer was that the testimony within forbade him to take the oath." This letter shows that even then, six years after joining the

---

* Eleventh Month (Jan.).

† John Barwick (1612-1664), Canon of Durham, and Dean of St. Paul's, a royalist high churchman of unblemished reputation, was appointed about this time to visit the bishops, and obtain their opinion about the episcopal succession. He declined to accept a mitre, lest it should be said his anxiety to maintain this arose from personal hopes.

Society, Crisp was looked upon as one of its leaders.

In Feb. 1662, Crisp was apprehended at a meeting in a private house at Harwich, and committed with Mary Vanderwall of Harwich, Edward Boyce, and William Martin to prison there.   They wrote a paper dated from Harwich Common Gaol (No. 73), protesting against the illegality of the proceeding, the mittimus having been written before their examination.   The exact term of their imprisonment has not been ascertained, but on 25th Sept., Crisp was still there, and wrote two letters to Justice Eldred, of Olivers, Stanway, near Colchester (App. B., Nos. 23, 24).

In 1663 a vehement persecution of the Friends took place in Colchester, under William Moore, Mayor, who, during two years of office, imprisoned more than sixty in the Moot Hall. These must have consisted of Colchester Friends, or those visiting the town, for while all Friends from other parts of Essex were confined in the Castle, which was the county gaol, the townsmen of Colchester were committed by the Mayor to the Moot Hall, it being the borough prison.   The remains of this building were to be seen forty years ago.   The drawing facing p. xl. shows the entrance to the cells, situated in the keep of the Castle, where Frances Marriage, Andrew Smith, and John Child, of Felstead, with many others, both men and women, were confined.   The irons still remain *in situ* in the damp, dark prison, about which, in spite of the whitewashed walls, one can hardly find the way.

From the 25th October throughout the entire winter, the persecution in Colchester raged.   The meeting-houses were closed and barricaded, but the Friends assembled outside. They were forcibly dispersed by troopers, they gathered again as usual.   In Crœse's "History of the Quakers," 1696, and Besse's "Sufferings," vol. i., pp. 199, 200, a full account is to be found.   Crisp was one of the first arrested, and he remained about a year in prison.   A letter which is not dated, but which was probably written a few weeks after his arrest, to the new Mayor, as it greets him as "the ruler of a great and mighty people," must have sufficiently shown William Moore what manner of people he had to deal with. "It is not thy frowns nor threats, thy imprisoning nor amerciaments, that can deter us . . . I tell thee thou hast a people to deal withal in this town, whose God and worship is dearer to them than their natural lives. And if thou shouldst so shut them up, and deprive them of that comfort to their outward man, which God allows, and nature requires, as to bring any to the laying down their lives for their Testimony, yet the thing which thou strikest at will still flourish more and more." ("Works," p. 112). On the 10th February, 1664, Caton writes to Crisp from Yarmouth prison (No. 137), condoling with him on his bonds. On the 1st October, 1664, Steven addressed a letter to the Mayor, in which he states he has been forty-eight weeks in the Moot Hall ("Works," p. 109). Some had been there even longer, for he says :—"Thou art now the third Mayor in this town, since some of us were committed to prison, for no other thing than being at a peaceable meeting of the people of God. And one leaves them bound, and another leaves them bound, and now it is the work that lies before thee to unloose the unjust bonds of the innocent."

It is somewhat remarkable that during Moore's fourth mayoralty, in 1692, a deed, dated 20th July, 1692, was executed with his signature, under an Act entitled, "An Act for exempting his Majesty's subjects, Dissenters from the Church of England, from the penalties of certain lands," by which the Meeting-house in St. Martin's Lane was absolved from the payment of taxes. This was effected by Crisp's intervention, who, as is recorded in the minute book at Colchester, "prosecuted the case at Quarter Sessions, with attorney," and the objection was allowed, under the returns of the court held 10th December, 1689.

In 1668, Crisp was again in prison, this time at Ispwich. The imprisonment lasted for some months, and the time was employed by him in writing his " Plain Pathway opened," published the same year. This is the last time that he was imprisoned, and indeed an easier time was soon to begin for this much enduring body. The last record affecting Crisp, of which we have particulars in Besse's "Sufferings," is of his being fined £20 at a meeting at Horsleydown on the 19th June, 1670. This was the sum imposed on the preacher in all nonconformist conventicles for a first offence. It was probably paid by some of his friends, either in goods or money, since Crisp himself was not imprisoned at that time. The fine for the second offence was £40, the person in whose house the meeting was held was fined £20, and each person present 10s.

It will be seen by a reference to the notes on the Mennonites, &c., pp. 16, 27, that there existed in Holland and Germany before the time of Fox, various bodies holding some similar tenets to those of which he was the first expounder in England. The introduction of quakerism into Holland followed shortly after the rise of the Society here. Among the earliest converts of Edward Burrough, and Francis Howgil, was William Ames. He was born in Somersetshire, and having been a Baptist preacher, was serving in the Parliamentary Army at Cork in 1655, when he heard these two first coadjutors of Fox. Two years after, he settled in Amsterdam, and became the pioneer of quakerism in Holland, being shortly followed by John Stubbs and William Caton.

In the same year, 1657, the Friends by their zeal in street-preaching, &c., attracted the attention of the Magistrates in Rotterdam, and eight of the most troublesome were put in prison. Their numbers continued steadily to increase. On the 8th June, 1675, the Rotterdam Friends applied to the Magistrates to protect them from the populace, by whom they were molested during the hours of service. After a second application, the reply was given them, that they should never obtain leave to assemble within the jurisdiction of the city. The Friends replied " that they would never solicit from the magistracy of Rotterdam, or from any civil power in the world, permission to meet in private for the purpose of serving God in spirit and truth, and that therefore they would continue to assemble as formerly." (Steven's Hist. of the Scotch Church in Rotterdam. Edin., 1832, p. 337). No further notice was taken of them. The meetings were held in private houses, and towards the end of the seventeenth century, a house was purchased on the South Blaak, Rotterdam, which was sold in 1725, being described in the title deeds as the "Meeting-house of the Friends," *Quakers Vergaderplaats*. In 1786, five merchants of Amsterdam bought, in the name of the Society of Friends of London, a small house on the north side of the Wine Street, which they fitted up as a Meeting-house. The numbers afterwards gradually decreased, and for some years there has not been a Quaker in Holland, that we are aware of. The discovery of any of the lost registers of that country, would be a most interesting one to the student of early Quaker history.

It was no doubt Crisp's business connections with the Dutch that first turned his attention to that country, and in 1663 he paid his first visit there. "This," he says, in his Journal, "I did with cheerfulness ; and though in an unknown land, and with an unknown speech, yet by an interpreter sometimes, and sometimes in my own tongue, I declared the Truth to the refreshing of many, and to the bringing back some from error ; and having accomplished that visit I returned in peace to England." He next travelled in the North of England, and afterwards laboured in London, of the wickedness of which city he seemed distressfully convinced, and saw in the visitations of the plague, and the fire of 1666, judgments upon the same. In 1667, he again went to Holland, this time accompanied by Josiah Coale. They spent about three months there, and almost immediately on his return, Crisp went down to the North of England. By this time, he had accepted his position. He found himself led "to and fro from country to country, not out of constraint now, but of a willing mind, and free from the cares of this life." This may be taken to mean that he had probably disposed of his business, or, at any rate, arranged for its being carried on independently of himself.

From this time, he says "the weight and care of the affairs of the Lords people in the Low Countries pressed more and more heavily upon me." In 1669, we find him setting forth again to visit them. He was now able to preach to them in their own tongue, so that he was encouraged to proceed still farther in his travels, and passing through Friesland, he entered Germany, and reached Griesheim, near Worms, where he found a body of people who had for some ten years suffered various distresses. They were just at that time in fresh tribulation, owing to a fine imposed by the Palsgrave, of four rix dollars a year, for each family attending meetings other than those established by law. Upon their declining to pay this, goods to a far larger amount were taken from them, and they found themselves in great need. In No. 76, Crisp relates how from five persons a sum amounting to £28 15s. English money, was taken. The Mennonites having consented to the fine, the Friends, he says, were left to suffer alone. But "this spoyle they endured with joy, rather than . . . . purchase spiritual freedom from carnal men." Crisp at once proceeded to Heidelberg, where he had a friendly interview with Charles Louis, the Elector Palatine, and the fine was ultimately removed. Crisp returned to Groningen, and thence to Amsterdam, where many strangers flocked to his meetings, when they found him speaking without an interpreter. Jan Claus, however, accompanied him. He acted as interpreter on many occasions to Friends travelling, and says he studied much that he might qualify himself for this labour (Kendall's Letters, p. 48.) The Diary kept during this visit to Holland will be found in the Collection, No. 76. "A briefe Journall of my travels into Germany," &c. The principal event of this journey was that through his assistance, a business or "discipline" meeting was satisfactorily set up.

Upon returning to England, Crisp proceeded to the West, where he had never yet been. He went, with many stoppages, to the Land's End, thence home by Portsmouth, Hampshire, and London. The Diary of this journey (No. 15) is here given as an evidence of Crisp's indefatigable zeal. He was at that time aged forty-one.

"A BRIEFE JOURNALL OF MY JOURNEY INTO YE WEST OF ENGLAND,
SAM. CATER BEING MY COMPANION.

On ye 27th of ye 8th Mo. [Oct.], 1669, we went from London to Stanes, to Richard Ashfields.

28 ditto. We had a meeting at Longford, nr Colbrooke.

29 ditto. We went to Reading.

30 — We had a meeting there in ye prison.

1 of ye 10 Mo. [Dec.] We had a meeting at Samuel Burgeses, by Williamton [Williamscote].

2 ditto. A meeting at Edmund Hides at Blewberry.

3 — At William Westons, at Oare.

4 — We went to Bart[ho]lmew Malams at Lambourne.

5 — We had a meeting there, it being a first day of ye week.

6 — We had a meeting at Marlborow, at Wm. Hitchcocks.

7 — We had a meeting at Calne, at Arther Ismaeds.

8 — We had a meeting at Headington, at John Rogers.

— And the same night another at Chippenham, at Thos. Neats.

9 — We had a meeting at Holinton, at Tho. Colmans.

10 — We had a meeting at Slatenford [Slaughterford] at Elizabeth Wallises.

11 — We went into Bristol.

12 — We had meetings there.

13 — We were at ye mens meeting there.

14 — We had a meeting at Winterburne, at Thomas Hills.

15 — We had a meeting at Oldson, and returned to Tho. Hills.

16,17,18 We staid at Bristoll, and were refreshed in the Lords abundant goodness to his people there, and were a refreshing to them.

19 — We left them and went to Bath.

20 — We had a meeting there.

21 — We went to Katherine Evans house.

22 — We went to Glasenbury.

23 — We had a meeting there.

24 — We had a meeting at Taunton.

25 — We mett Tho. Salthouse, and had a meeting at Sanford.

26 — Tho. Salthouse and I had a meeting at Columpton, and same at Topsham.

27 — We mett at Exeter, and travelled to Crockernwell.

28 — We went to Lanston [Launceston], and had a meeting there.

29 — We went to Tree[s]mer, to Humphrey Lowers.

30 — We continued there.

31 — We went to Redruth.

1st day 11th Mo. [Jan. 1670]. We came to Bra[y] neere ye Lands End, at John Ellises.

2 day. We had a meeting there, [it] being 1st day.

3 — Wo walked to ye Lands End.

4 — We travelled to Helston, where Robinson ye persecutor dyed by his bull.

5 — We had a meeting at Kenence [Kynance] near ye lizard land.

6 — We had a meeting at Bethick, neer Falmouth.

7 — We went to Truro, and so to Tregonsenes.

8 & 9 We staid there, and had a meeting on ye 9, being 1st day.

10 — Wo went to Bodmin, and so to Tree[s]mere.

11 — We had a meeting at Tree[s]mere, and then we parted.

12 — I had a meeting at Tho: Mounts, neere Liskard.

13 — I came to Plymouth, and had a meeting there.

14, 15, 16 I continued there, and there me[t] Thomas Salthouse againe, and we and friends were mutually refreshed one in another.

18 — I went and had a meeting at Batten, and went to Kingsbridge

19 — I went from thence to Totnes, and soe to Exeter.

20 — I had a meeting at Topsham.

21 — I had a meeting at Memb[u]ry.

22 — I went to Gregory Stoake.

23 — I had a great meeting there.

24 — I went to Thorncomb.

25 — I had a meeting at Bridport.

26 — I had a meeting at Weymouth.

27 — I went to Poole.

28 — I had a meeting there.

29 — I went to Ringwood, and soe to Southampton.

30 — I had a meeting there, [it] being 1st day.

31 — I went to Portsmouth, and had a meeting there.

1st of yᵉ 12th month [Feb.]   1 went to Swanmore, and had a meeting, and then to Winchester.

2 — I had a meeting at Andover.

3 — I had a meeting at Al[re]sford.

4 — I had a meeting at Alton.

5 — I went home with Steven Smith in Surrey.

6 — I had a meeting at John Smiths neere Gilford.

7 — I returned to London, and staid there four days.

8 — I returned to Colchester to my wife and relations, to our mutuall joy and refreshment in yᵉ lord ; who hath both preserved and supported me in this long journey in places where I had not before travelled, therefore to him be the praise and glory for ever."

Steven Crisp

In March, 1670, he was committed to Ipswich gaol for being present at a Conventicle, but was released at the end of three months, and in July he started off again for Holland. Taking Peter Hendricks, from whom there are seven letters, as his companion, he this time reached the borders of Sweden and Denmark, visiting Hamburgh, and towns in the Duchy of Holstein. At Frederikstadt they were well received, and their meetings grew so large, that the attention of various Professors and Teachers was aroused, and one Eppinghooft, with others, desired a public dispute with them. "An Answer to Five Questions set forth by L. Hendricks Eppenhoof (or Eppenhooft)," was written by Jacob Jacobs, and published 1670 (Smith's Biblio. Anti. Quak., p. 168). After distributing books and papers, they returned by boat to Bremen, thence to Oldeburg and Embden. At this place, there was a considerable number of people who, from about the year 1662, had professed quakerism, and who had been, and continued to be, ruthlessly hunted out by the authorities until the year 1686, when, as we learn by Sewel (vol. ii. p. 321), an order was issued by the Senate, dated 25th March 1686, for their admission and protection in the city, "in their free trade and exercise of religion." This was done in answer to an appeal signed by the same five persons whose names are appended to No. 23, with those of Sewel and Crisp in addition.

The travellers next proceeded to Leeuwarden in Friesland. Here three Friends of Amsterdam were in prison, with orders that none should see them, but Crisp, with his usual success, applied for and obtained leave to visit them, and afterwards departed for Amsterdam, where he arrived about the beginning of November. After looking up the fraternity in Alkmaer, Haarlem, Rotterdam and other towns, he returned to England, and spent three or four months travelling in the Southern counties. His many correspondents, however, kept him fully informed of what was going on in Holland, and he shortly became convinced that his presence there was once more required. Certain disorderly spirits having arisen amongst them, and refusing to conform to the counsel of the Friends, they were finally testified against in the papers, Nos. 45ᵃ, 45ᵇ, and 46 of the present Collection. Having settled matters in Holland, where he had come to be looked up to almost as a bishop of one of our outlying colonies might be at the present day, Steven Crisp returned to England in June, 1671, and was "much rejoiced to see the peace, unity, and courage among the people . . . after their sore persecution." He returned to Colchester, where he was very ill for a time, but on recovering, he, nothing daunted, again set off for Yorkshire and Durham, where he had not been, he says, for three or four years, "by reason of his being so much beyond the sea." His companion for part of this journey was Samuel Cater, who also had first heard of Quakerism from James Parnel (see p. 5). The winter, he records, was "very sharp," and his body "through much affliction, very crazy," so that when he returned, about February 1672, to Colchester, it was "to the great joy of my poor wife and friends who had longings for my return, as I had again to see their faces." He

o

remained in England, about his home, until midsummer, and
then again sailed for the Low countries, where he spent
about three months. While there, he published " An
Address to the Rulers and Inhabitants in Holland and
the rest of the United Provinces," which is to be found
in his printed works, edited by Field (Lond. 1694.) Six
months were next passed in active labours in and around
Colchester, and then Steven Crisp started off again to Embden,
where the Friends were still in much suffering. Crisp was
received by Dr. Hasbert, a physician of that town, who was
the chief member of the community, and at whose house
their meetings were held. In " The Sufferings of Friends at
Embden," No. 156, a full account will be found of Dr.
Hasbert's repeated imprisonments and banishments from
Embden, and of his death at Amsterdam, $\frac{7}{8}$ of September,
1676. He is continually mentioned by Fox in his Journal,
being styled always " the father-in-law of Jan Claus," who
at the time was acting as Fox's interpreter.

About this time, Crisp undertook what must have been to
him a labour of love, viz., the writing of a *Testimony* as a
Preface to the Works of James Parnel (published 1675).
After giving a graphic description of the " darkness and
sorrow of those days," from which we have seen that he,
mainly through Parnel's preaching, emerged, he tells how
this " faithful messenger " arose, and brought a deliverance
to many whose hearts were ready to faint. After narrating
the circumstances of Parnel's life and death, he concludes :
—" Thus, dearest Reader, have I given thee a brief account
of this dear Plant of God, and of his blessed Fruit, some
whereof thou mayest find in this following Book, which if
read in sincerity and uprightness of heart, will tend to thy
benefit."

Crisp continued to visit Holland year by year, and in the
intervals, he found time to go into Yorkshire, Bristol, and
other parts of England. He also was present at the Yearly
Meetings, and after that of 1678, he returned to Colchester,

and "set his own house in order," preparatory to going once more to Holland in the autumn of the same year. He had not proceeded very far up the Rhine, when he was overtaken with sickness, and was carried in a weak state on board a boat, in which he was conveyed down to Rotterdam, and thence to his own home, in a state of prostration and suffering from a long-standing complaint. The next summer was the first he had missed paying his annual visit to Holland, since 1663. In 1680 he was again in Friesland, and this time proceeded to Crefeld, where he spent three days.

Soon after reaching home in September, he had a bad attack of fever, which brought him very near the grave, but he says "to live or to die I was contented." The fever abated, and he was restored to health, though he spent most of that winter in Essex, but in the spring he once more set out for Yorkshire and the north, where he stayed "till about harvest time," when he returned to London, and so home. "And by this time," he says, "I was again overtaken with great pains of the stone, and other distempers, which brought my body very low, and little was expected by any but my departure." By December, however, he was able to go to his Quarterly Meeting, and afterwards to visit Harwich and Ipswich, but most of the winter was spent near home. The next year, after attending the Yearly Meeting in London, he started for the one at Amsterdam, which was arranged to be held three weeks later. He was accompanied by many Friends from Dantzic, Holstein, Hamburg, &c., who had been at the London Yearly Meeting.

It may be interesting to state here that in the early days of the Society, circulating Yearly or "General" Meetings were held in different parts of the country. A Yearly Meeting's Epistle to the counties, &c., was issued annually, the first being dated May 1666, and bearing among others, Crisp's signature. But at a meeting held at Devonshire House, 29th May 1672, it was agreed that "a general meeting be held once a year, in the week called Whitsun week," in London.

From that year until the present, this meeting has been regularly held on this now historic site.

On his arrival in Holland, Steven Crisp was seized with so violent an attack of his disorder, that he found himself too weak for travelling, and in June 1683, he returned home. Not long after, in the middle of November, his wife Dorothy Crisp died. " She had been," he says, " a meet help, and a faithful and loving wife to me about five and thirty years." She was fifty-eight years old, and was buried on the 22nd Nov. in the graveyard in Almshouse Lane.

From various entries in the old " Two weeks meeting " and other books at Colchester, we see that Crisp was kept busily employed in the affairs of his church. Thus, he acted as executor to William Marlow, of Harwich, and trustee to his daughter Grace. He held the indentures of apprenticeship of the three children of his relative Elizabeth Crisp, of St. Osyth, and managed the residue of her estate for their benefit. He was ordered to remit to London the monies collected in Colchester, &c., for the relief of the Friends imprisoned by the Turks, in Algiers. He received, 24th July, 1682, on the completion of the gallery agreed to be made at the east end of the Colchester Meeting-house, the sum of £12 2s. 6d., which he had disbursed for the expenses of the same. And he frequently acted as clerk to the above meeting, many of the minutes of which are in his handwriting, as for instance, under date 24th of 4th mo. (June), 1672.

It is time now to give some account of the Dericks or Dirrix family, with whom Crisp had been for many years in intimate relations. The three sisters, Neisy, Gertrude, and Annekin, appear to have occupied a considerable position in Amsterdam. They were wealthy, cultivated, and universally admired, and all became quakers. Neisy Dericks, the elder sister, by her will, allusions to which will be found in No. 60, left for the use of the Friends in Amsterdam, certain sums of money, which she had out at interest. Some dispute arising between her executors, Jan Claus and Steven Crisp were appointed arbitrators. Neisy Dericks seems to have been highly esteemed by all who knew her, and she is thus spoken of by William Caton. (Journal, 1689, p. 71) :—

" I received some letters out of Holland, whereby I was informed of the death of Niesie Dirricks, of Amsterdam, who had been a dear and special friend of mine, and a true and faithful servant to the flock of God in the low countries, of whose love and virtue, faithfulness and good service which she did in her day, a volume might be written. When I heard of her departure, my heart was much saddened and broken within me, and indeed it was more than I well could bear."

Others, too, bear testimony to her excellence. Besse relates (vol. ii., p. 455) that in 1661, Neisy Dericks was cited before the magistrates for selling quaker books, and although there appeared no law against this, she was fined £30, the magistrates deciding that the books were seditious, without reading them.

Annekin Dericks, the third sister, became the wife of William Caton, and in his "Journal" (Lond. 1689), he tells the story of their courtship with a charming *naïveté*. We should like to reproduce it entirely in his own words, but for want of space, we must be satisfied with extracts. We have read his expressions of sorrow at the death of the elder sister Neisy, and it was not long after, that the idea came into his mind how " helpful he might be to Annekin in the service which he foresaw would be required of her," now that she had lost the sister who had been her right hand. "Night and day," he says, "for a pretty long time, did abundance of objections come into my mind concerning it, but withal matter sufficient to answer them all." So at length he " began to acquiesce," but he "did not once open his mouth to any, for the space of many months." In this deliberate manner, and with this solemn " seeking for guidance," does he proceed, true to the first quaker principle of " the Inner Light." But he was anxious for the confirmation of his notion that it was right, and perhaps too, for the approbation of his fellow-members, for it would be a painful thing to incur their rebukes ; so he decided before speaking to the lady, to lay it before some of "the brethren," and if they "own" it, to be satisfied. Six months more of his labours in Germany, and he began to feel drawings in his heart back towards Holland. He records their meeting in the simple words "and as for Annekin, her Love abounded towards me, and mine did the like to her in the Lord."

Everything seemed to go smoothly, the brethren approved, and "in a certain time, when he had a convenient opportunty," William began to tell her in "great humility and fear," yet with manly straightforwardness, what was in his heart. Three things he had to propound to her, which he desired to leave to her consideration, and in due time to have her answer :—

" *The first* was, it was upon me to give her to understand, that as for the matter of *estate* mine was not like unto hers, for I had not much as to the outward. And she was to consider whether, notwithstanding, she could consent to this thing.

" *Secondly*, she was to consider how I should expect my liberty (which was more to me than the treasures of Egypt) to go abroad in the service of the Lord, as I had done before, whether it was to visit Friends, or upon any other Service for the Lord, or upon the Truth's account ; this she was also to consider beforehand, that when the thing came to pass, it might not seem strange to her.

" *Thirdly*, she was to consider how if the thing should come to pass, there might peradventure follow some trouble, either from the magistrates or from some of her relations. . . . Therefore she was to consider whether she could bear that or no."

Caton is here of course alluding to the uncertainty whether marriages solemnized according to quaker usages, would be recognised as legal or not. As a matter of fact, twenty years later (see Nos. 1, 10, 83, and 94), the question was again raised, but satisfactorily settled. In "several weeks," for everything must be done with due quaker deliberation, Annekin returned him her answer.

"And as to the first she said, it was not means which she looked after, but vertue. And as to the second she said, that when I was moved of the Lord to go upon any service on the account of truth, she hoped that she should not be the woman that should hinder me upon such an account. And as to the last she said, that if the Lord did once bring the thing so far as to be effected, she hoped that to bear what people without should say, would be one of the least crosses."

For the pair had resolved that theirs should be the first marriage celebrated according to the practices of the Society. Annekin, some time after, opened her heart to her betrothed, and told him that while he was in Germany, an intimation of the future had come over her, and that she had longed for, and yet dreaded, his return. After they had again "waited," and several months had expired, Annekin went to him one day in a state of pious exaltation. "She was exceedingly broken, and wept in an excessive manner. It was upon her to give herself up to the will of the Lord, and she was moved to speak these words, *Wy zyn niet meer twee maer een vleeze.* "We are no more twain but one flesh." When William heard her speak these words with a flood of tears, he was "something moved, and the life in him began to arise, saying she is the gift of God to thee." So now their consciences were entirely at rest, and he proceeded to publish their intention three times in the meeting at Amsterdam, as well as in his old nurture-place of Swarthmoor. Of this meeting he was still a member. On the last day of October 1662, they were married at Amsterdam, before a General Meeting of Friends, in the simple quaker form. The same afternoon, the body of William Ames, the first quaker to settle in Holland, was laid in the grave, with labour and anxiety on the part of the Friends, the rude and curious people being very tumultuous. A serious ending to a wedding, but those were serious times.

Gertrude Dericks, the second sister, had married a wealthy Dutchman, named Adrian Van Losevelt. Frequent mention of him is made in Caton's letters, Nos. 134-142, and he seems to have been regarded by Gertrude's friends, as a rather shallow sort of person, a doubtful help to his wife. In one of Caton's chatty letters, dated 11th Nov., 1664, he speaks of him in plain terms. "Adrian is much as he was, inconstant and fickle, little as yet seasoned with truth. Deare Gertie loves the truth and Friends in her very heart, but is often bowed down with burdens like she was groaning under when thou wast here." Crisp had spoken words to her in a time of great tribulation, which she had never forgotten, and all visitors from England were warmly welcomed for his sake.

Letters also passed between them, although unfortunately none are preserved in this Collection. In John Kendall's "Letters of I. Penington, and Miscellaneous Letters," London, 1796, pp. 128, 9, are two letters, which though neither dated nor addressed by name, are in all probability written by Steven Crisp to Gertrude. Kendall, although he does not state his source, says they are published for the first time, and as they occur among other letters drawn from the Crisp Collection, it is possible that the originals may have then formed a part of it.* At any rate there is no doubt that the valuable books and papers left by John Kendall to the school partially endowed by him at Lexden, would have afforded information as to Crisp's labours in Holland, and the history of the Dutch quakers. These, however, being found unserviceable for the use of the school, were by consent of the Charity Commissioners, sold in 1865.

One of the two letters is here given, as eminently characteristic of the spirit which possessed Steven Crisp.

" Dearly beloved,

In the Lord my soul salutes thee, as one who is brought into my remembrance, by that spirit that doth often bow me to thy burdens, which I know are not few.

Dear heart, it is nothing but the day that expels the night, and the day star brings the hope thereof ; therefore, my dear friend, for as much

---

* In the Appendix to the Report bound with the Collection, is a list of seven papers belonging to it previous to 1835, of which this is one.

[From a pen and ink drawing.]

Door of the prison in Colchester Castle,
where the Essex Friends were confined, 1655-70.

as it hath pleased God to cause this star to appear, and that thou knowest thine eye has seen it, be not discouraged because of clouds, but know that the day is at hand. And as concerning all Satans buffetings, know and consider that though they are never so many and strong, yet they are but like the waves of the sea, and they are limited ; feel thou an habitation in that which limits them, and rest in patience ; and possess thy soul in that, and it will be well in the end ; if there were no trials, there would not be so much need of patience. Dear Heart, feel my love, which is beyond words.

So, with my dear love to thy husband, and Anna [Caton], &c., I rest thy true friend."

Steuen Crisp

The Losevelts occupied a house in the Vish-steege, Amsterdam until about September 1663, when they moved to a much larger one with a rental of "about five or six hundred gilders a year." This sum would equal about £50. Here, on the occasion of the first official visit of any members of the Society to Holland, William Penn was lodged, and here, on the 2nd August 1667, a General Meeting was held, at which George Fox, Robert Barclay, William Penn, John and Benjamin Furly, George Keith, and many others were present. They explained to the Dutch community "the benefit and service of Yearly, Quarterly, and Monthly Meetings of men and women." (Fox's "Journal," 1765, p. 501. Penn's "Travels in Germany," ed. Barclay, p. 4.) The next day a more public meeting was held, also in Gertrude's house. At this "many professors of several sorts were present." In the afternoon there was another meeting, "more private." The day following, a meeting of Friends only, "wherein by joint agreement was settled" the order and arrangement of the several meetings for discipline in Holland and Germany. The next day being Sunday, Fox says, "we had a very large meeting, there coming to it a great concourse of people of several opinions, Baptists,

Seekers, Socinians, Brownists, and some of the Collegians.*
Robert Barclay, George Keith, William Penn and I, did all
severally declare the everlasting truth among them, . . .
and the meeting ended quietly and well."

The day after, Fox started for his tour in Holland and Germany. Being unable to proceed so far as Heidelberg, he wrote an
Epistle to the Princess Elizabeth, with whom he had already
had some correspondence, and sent it by the hands of three
quaker women, Isabel Yeomans his step-daughter, George
Keith's wife, and Gertrude Dericks, who had visited the
Princess the year before with Elizabeth Hendricks, the writer
of No. 70. They were received with much grace, and in
writing to Penn some time later, the Princess affectionately
mentions "dear Gertrude."

Fox returned to Amsterdam at midnight on the 12th September. The gates of the city being shut, he and his party lay on
board the vessel till the morning, when they went to Gertrude's
house, and were warmly welcomed on their safe return. The
next two or three weeks were spent by Fox at Amsterdam, with
occasional visits to the neghbouring towns. Upon one visit
to Haarlem, he records Peter Hendricks and Gertude as his
companions, and says that the latter interpreted for him
for several hours, while he "declared the truth." A large
discussion was also held with some priests, and upon William
Penn's return, a famous dispute with Galenus Abrahamsz†
took place. It lasted for several days, and was sustained
chiefly in Latin. All these gatherings took place at
Gertrude's house.

On the 21st of October, she and her two children set sail
with Penn, Fox, and others, to return to England. They were
three days and two nights at sea, and upon landing at Harwich,
they proceeded to Colchester, in which place Fox stayed long
enough to hold, on the Sunday following, a "large and

---

* Or Collegianten. See p. 16.

† Galenus Abrahamsz, a famous Baptist preacher and doctor. See p. 64.

weighty " meeting, at which he calculates " over a thousand people, Friends and townspeople," were present. Having heard of his return from Holland, they flocked in from several parts of the country.

Gertrude and her children repaired to the house of Steven Crisp, on a visit to him and his wife, of several weeks' duration. On the 29th Nov. following, she wrote an *Epistle* dated from Colchester to Friends, printed, no date. This Epistle is mentioned by Rous in his letter to Crisp, dated Barbadoes, May 1679, as read by the Friends there with much pleasure. This was Gertrude's first visit to Colchester, but several years after, when she was a widow (though we have no account of her husband's death), she again went over, accompanied by her sister Annekin, and spent many weeks in the house of Crisp and his wife. Indeed it seems probable that she was there at the time of Dorothy Crisp's death, for in the letter to Penn, No. 24, dated 4th May 1684, a few months after that event, Steven Crisp says :—" Our dear Gertrude is still here, a careful nurse to me."

Towards the end of that year, 1684, Crisp became satisfied that Gertrude was to be his wife, and the next spring, after attending the Yearly Meeting in London together, they started, accompanied by many Friends, both Dutch and English, for Holland, to attend the Amsterdam gathering. Early in August, they returned to Colchester, and on the 31st, Crisp announced to his Monthly Meeting his intention of marriage.

Simple as the quaker marriage ceremony is and always was, the formalities preceding it, were, at this time, both elaborate and precise. Twice was the intention to be personally announced, both to the men's and women's meetings, each of which appointed two persons to enquire if both the parties were free of all other engagements. When final consent was given, the care and authority of the meeting proceeded still farther in the case of a widow with children, viz., to the ascertaining that a due proportion of her late husband's property was settled upon his children. This wise and just

rule was early insisted upon by Fox, and is laid down by
him in Canon IV. of "The Canons and Institutions," 1669.
In his own case, as is well known, Mrs. Fell's considerable
property was entirely made over to her seven daughters and
one son, upon her marriage. That this was also done in
Crisp's case, will be seen by a reference to the early minute
book of the Colchester Meeting.

The following entries from "The Women's Meeting Book
for the town of Colchester," are interesting.

" Coulchester, the 7th day of the 7th month [Sept.], 1685.

This day, came Steven Crisp and Gertrit Derrix to our meeting, and
acquainted frinds with their intention of marage, and this metting
desires Ann Ffurly and Ann Talcot to Inquire if she is clere from all
others, and to give an account to this metting.

" The 21st of the 7th month, 1685.

This day, came Steven Crisp and Geertruyd Dircks to our meeting the
2 time, and acquainted frindes with thair intentions of taking each
other in marage, and this meeting finding nothing but that thay are cleare
from all others, this meeting desired Ann Furly and Ann Tailcoat to
signify the same to the man's meeting."

Gertrude Dericks seems to have dropped her husband's
name of Losevelt, in accordance with an old custom in
Holland and, at one time, in Scotland. In Smith's "Catalogue " she is apparently confounded with her sister, Niesy
Dericks. She is spoken of by Fox and others (Nos. 28 and
99 of this Collection) as Gertrude Dericks Niesen. Under
this name, her marriage is entered in the Colchester Friends'
register. It took place at Colchester, on the 1st of October,
1685.

On the 18th of May following, Gertrude's son, Cornelis
Losevelt, was also married at Colchester, to Abigail Furly,
daughter of John Furly, the son of John Furly, linendraper, of
St. Runwald's parish, Alderman in 1637, and Mayor of Col-
chester in 1650. Cornelis and Abigail Losevelt's daughter
Gertrude is mentioned by Crisp in his will. The absence

of any further information in the Colchester registers, leads to the conclusion that Cornelis Losevelt returned to Rotterdam after his mother's death. Cornelis Dericks, or Derrix, who occupied the position of deacon in the Scottish Church at Rotterdam, from 1748 to 1752, was probably a relation. (Steven's "History of the Scottish Church at Rotterdam," Edin., 1832, p. 370).

The marriage of Steven Crisp with Gertrude seems to have been a supremely happy one, in spite of the couple being both well advanced in years. We can imagine his distress, when, after only two years of companionship crowning their long friendship, he had again to part with her. She died at Colchester, after a short illness, on the 9th May 1687, and was buried on the 11th, in the Chapel Graveyard, Almshouse Lane.

Gertrude Crisp was a woman spoken of with warmest affection, and praise, by all who knew her. Her husband's tribute in his Journal (Works, ed. Field, 1694, p. 58) is worth preserving, " Indeed," he says, " she was a woman beyond many, excelling in the vertues of the Holy Spirit with which she was baptized, as she shewed forth both in life and doctrine, which made her to be a sweet savour throughout the churches of Christ, and was a pattern of Patience and Holiness, discharging her Place as a tender and watchful Mother to her children, and as a careful and loving wife to me. But alas as the greatest enjoyments of Temporal blessings have their end, so it happened unto me, for it proved the pleasure of the Lord to try me whether I could part with, as well as receive, this great Mercy ; for in the beginning of the year 1687, she fell into Bodily Weakness, and continued so two or three months, and upon the ninth of the third month [May], she slept with the Faithful in the Lord, in a perfect Resignation to his will, making a blessed end, to my great joy and consolation. For although it was hard to Flesh and Blood to part with so precious a Companion, and to be left alone in my old age, accompanied with many In-

firmities of Body, yet feeling fellowship with her in the joy
into which she is entred, gives me great satisfaction, knowing right well her portion is with the Righteous."

When he had buried her, Crisp went up to London, and as
he quaintly puts it, "conversed among the brethren for three
months." This companionship soothed and solaced him in
his grief. He returned to Colchester for the winter, and the
next year, was more than once in London on important affairs,
for he had long become a recognised leader of the Society. In
1688, when James II. was anxious to conciliate the Dissenters,
Crisp was, by royal command, offered the Commission of the
Peace. Sewel says, " He was much too circumspect, to be
caught thus." At any rate the honour was declined, but from
the fact of its being made, and from the contents of No. 45,
which relates to the sale of timber in Great Bryan's Wood, by
Crisp, we gather that he was a landed proprietor, more or less.
The wood may have been in Great Tey parish, a certain Sir
Francis Bryan having held property there a little earlier.

In the year 1690 Crisp wrote a long " Epistle of love and
brotherly advice to all the Churches of Christ throughout
the World," which Sewel prints in his History (vol. ii. p.
358). It is dated from London, 15th Nov. Not many months
after, on 13th Jan. 1691, George Fox died, at Henry Gouldney's
house in White Hart Court. Steven Crisp was with
him two hours before the end. He preached at the funeral,
the arrangements for which, and the great meetings held
afterwards, were largely of his making. Robert Barrow,
from whom we have letters in the present volume,
writing some last particulars down to Lancaster on the
day of the funeral, says : — " George shut up his eyes
himself, and his chin never fell nor needed any bind-
ing up, but he lay as if he had been fallen asleep. One
would have thought he smiled. He was the most pleasant
corpse I ever looked upon, and many hundreds of Friends
came to see his face, having the most part of three days time
to behold him before the coffin was nailed up. Friends

carried the coffin on their shoulders . without any bier, cloth or cover but the natural wood ; yet the coffin was very smooth and comely . . . I intended to go out of the city on the morrow after he began to be sick ; but seeing him ill, it was upon Friends mind I should stay . . . and I was glad to see such a heavenly and harmonious conclusion as dear George Fox made ; the sense and sweetness of it will I believe never depart from me." (Barclay's "Letters of Early Friends).

Shortly after George Fox's death, an order, dated 4th April, 1691, was sent down to the counties, signed by the thirteen Friends (of whom Crisp was one), appointed by Fox to see after the printing of his books, papers, epistles, and MSS. to " make search, and send up the titles, dates, and first and last sentence of each book, paper, or manuscript, that we may the better distinguish one from another, of all books. papers, or MSS., printed or written." This provided Steven Crisp with occupation for some time.

George Whitehead and Steven Crisp, with Penn and Barclay, both now rarely in London, the one being in Pennsylvania, the other in Scotland, from this time occupied the head of affairs in the Society, but as far as Crisp was concerned it was to be of short duration.

He was at the Yearly Meeting held in London from the 16th to the 19th of May 1692, and adds to the annual Epistle, the following postscript, signed by George Whitehead and himself, the contents of which are in extreme harmony with the prevailing spirit of his life, which was concord and agreement, though the outward events of it had been passed amidst war and revolutions. Born within three years of the accession of Charles I., he had seen the succession of six persons to the post of highest dignity in England, and had kept equally aloof from Kings, Queens, or Protectors.

" Dear friends,—With respect to our Antient and Innocent Testimony in the Foregoing Epistle, it is upon us further to add, viz., ' Away with those upbraiding characters of Jacobites and Williamites, Jemmites, and

Billites, &c., so used by the Worlds people one against another to make Parties and Divisions, and to stir up Wrath and Enmity. . . . And shew forth your affection to Christ, to his Kingdom and Government, by a quiet Life and peaceable subjection unto the higher Powers that God is pleased to set over us, which are at his disposing and not ours ; it being our Christian duty to desire their good, and to persuade them to what good we can for their safety, and our ease and relief, that in all Godliness and Honesty you may be innocently preserved out of all Offences, Reproach and Scandal, and all real occasions thereof.' "

As the summer advanced, Crisp's health again began to fail, but, zealous as ever, he preached at Devonshire House on the 17th July. This was his last sermon, and shows no sign of decaying intellect. But there was no question of return to his lonely home at Colchester, and at William Crouch's house, in Crown Court, Gracechurch Street, he was tenderly cared for. Finding that he grew rather worse, however, his friends removed him to William Crouch's country house at Wandsworth, four miles off, in the hope that the purer air would revive him. Field, in his Preface to the " Works," describes how "several Friends accompanied him on foot with the litter, lest there should be any want of assistance." On the 24th of August George Whitehead came to see him. He was very weak, yet lingering. " I see an end of mortality," he said to him, " yet cannot come at it. Dear George, I can live and die with thee." On the 27th, when George Whitehead again went down, he was nearer the end. " I hope I am gathering, I hope, I hope." The next day he died, and on the 31st his body was brought to Gracechurch Street Meeting House, and "borne on the shoulders of his friends and brethren that loved him," to the burial-place at Bunhill Fields, accompanied by a " great number of Friends and others." Many sermons were preached beside the grave of the good old man, who was loved by all, and left no enemy behind him.

Crisp had no near relations living at the time of his death. His own children had died young. I do not think he ever had a brother, and his sister, who had married John Hix, or Hicks, was dead. Her children are remembered with small presents in his will. His cousins Samuel, John, and Thomas Crisp, and their children, are all sharers in his means, and Samuel's son Steven is to be apprenticed if he will. There are small legacies to his various friends, and a touching tribute to his dearly-loved dead wife, in the bequest to her grand-daughter "Gertrude Losevelt, daughter of Cornelis Losevelt, when she shall have attained the age of sixteen years." Crisp's will as drawn up by himself, is a model of brevity and simplicity. It is not without interest, as characteristic of his time, and it is given in Appendix A.

We close this sketch with a slight review of Steven Crisp's literary work. It is not pretended to be a complete bibliography, since beyond one Dutch work, there is found nothing to add to the excellent list given by Joseph Smith in his "Catalogue," vol. i. pp. 466-477. The work named is "*De Gronden en Oorsaeken van de Ellende der Nederlanden ontdeckt, als mede de Middelen van derselver herstellinge aengewesen. Geschreven door een Liefhebber van haer Land*," &c., Amsterdam, 1672. "The Grounds and Causes of the Netherlands Misery discovered, likewise the Means to Remedy the same. Written by a lover of their Land," &c.

In 1694, John Field published "A Memorable Account of the Christian Experiences, Gospel Labours, Travels and Sufferings of that antient Servant of Christ, Steven Crisp," in which most of his writings are collected. He was a copious writer of Epistles and short addresses. Thirty-nine are included in the above. He seldom or never visited Holland without inditing an Epistle of love to the brethren who looked so eagerly for his visits, or of warning to the inhabitants of the towns where they had been so abused and insulted. Seven of these Dutch epistles are to be found in a curious thick quarto volume, with a printed title page, and MS. index under the title of "Collectio," published (no place), 1675.

The principal of Crisp's longer works is, " The Short History of a Long Travel from Babylon to Bethel," written in 1691, not many months before his death, the MSS. of which is in the present Collection.   It contains his spiritual auto-biography in the form of an allegory, written in terse yet graceful language, which contrasts favourably with the prolixity of the age. It was first published, Lond. 1711, and has been many times reprinted.   The twelfth edition was published, Manchester, 1841.

Several others of Crisp's writings ran through many editions, notably, " An Epistle to Friends concerning the Present and succeeding Times," first printed Lond. 1666, with preface by Margaret Fell to the third edition, 1679. Tenth ed. 1797 ; a " Plain Pathway opened to the Simple-hearted for the Answering all Doubts and Objections which do arise in them against the Light and Truth in the Inward Parts," 1668, translated into Dutch, 1669 ; and, " An Alarm sounded in the Borders of Egypt, which shall be heard in Babylon, and astonish the Inhabitants of the Defiled and Polluted Habita-tions of the Earth," &c., 1671. This was reprinted 1672, and 1691, and translated into High Dutch, Amsterdam, 1674.

His sermons preached in London between 25th April, 1688, and 17th July, 1692, were taken down in shorthand, and published by Nathaniel Crouch, who says he was "not of the Persuasion," in three vols., 1693, 4, under the title, " Several Sermons or Declarations of Mr. Steven Crisp, late of Colchester, in Essex, deceased. Exactly taken in Characters as they were delivered by him at the Publick Meeting Houses of the People called Quakers in Gracechurch St. and Devon-shire House, London. And now faithfully transcribed and published, together with the prayer at end of every sermon." These sermons seem to have been extremely popular, and were many times reprinted. Seventeen were translated by Sewel, and published Amsterdam, 1695.

Crisp's works became very popular in Holland, and most of them were translated into Dutch. Some, indeed, were written only to be translated, and were never published in English. Jan Claus, writing after Crisp's death to John Furly, under date Amsterdam, 11th Dec., 1693 (No. 132), says :—

"Concerning the bookes of deare S. Crisp, brother J. Rocloffs sayes he sente a Catalogue of em long agoe ; and indeed we have not kept a coppy of it, yᵗ I know, and to make another will require some more time then I have to spare at present, but it may be, there is a mistake in yᵉ case ; and if soe, then thou may know, Steven has not written one booke or paper in dutch (yᵗ is printed), but all first in English, and he used to keepe all his manuscripts to himselfe ; soe yᵗ thou maye finde among his Manuscripts a parcell of bookes yᵗ weare (I believe) never printed in English in his life time ; which relates some onely and some cheifely to this Countrie, and soe easily knowne. Yet I am willing to make another Catalogue of them, and send it thee when I have done soe."

This letter is another evidence of the care extended by the early quakers over all the literary efforts of their members. They had, from the beginning, realised the power of the press, and that the Yearly Meeting, in an authoritative manner, disseminated the literature of the body among all its subordinate meetings, will be seen by the following extracts from a book of MSS. Epistles at Colchester.

" Upon a complaint yᵗ yᵉ printer could not well carry on yᵉ charge of printing, with what number of booksformerly taken off his hands, agreed: That for yᵉ Incouragement of yᵉ printer and for yᵉ better dispersing of friends books, the proportions formerly settled, be augmented upon each county by one moiety more than formerly, viz., Essex, 37.°

" And also it was agreed that the Quarterly Meetings return yᵉ printer his money once a quarter, for his encouragement and assistance to carry on his business.

Dated the 20th and 21st of 3rd mo. [May], 1673."

Several manuscript works of Crisp in the present Collection, as well as one or two in the Devonshire House bundle, have apparently never been printed, but such of them as are

---

* [Twenty-seven had formerly been the number, the whole number of books taken off by the counties being 600.]

to be now obtained, especially "The Short History of a Long Travel," are well worth perusal. In the only life of Crisp hitherto published, by Samuel Tuke, York, 1824, many selections from his works are given, with some critical notices. This "Memoir" does not, however, furnish many particulars about his life, but if the reader derives half as much pleasure in following the events of this life, as I have in hunting out the same, I shall feel amply repaid.

The order of arrangement adopted in the Synopsis has been :—(1) A heading or title, stating the nature of the document, and if a letter, from whom to whom, with place if stated. (2) A Summary of the principal contents, if important, or in some cases, denoted by quotation marks, the entire letter or document. (3) Short biographies of the writers, recipients, or other persons mentioned in the letters or papers.

The MSS. having been numbered, and to some extent catalogued, by an official appointment of the Monthly Meeting some time before coming into the editor's hands, there was little choice but to follow the previous arrangment —somewhat haphazard and arbitrary—instead of the simple chronological order in which letters will be found placed, when several from one person occur. Those relating to the same subject have also been grouped together, and frequent references to other parts of the volume will be found, to assist the reader. The number of each document corresponding with the title in the Synopsis, will be found in the bottom left hand corner of the MSS. The folios are paged in the upper right hand corner.

As regards the dates used, it may not be known to the general reader that until the 31st Dec., 1751, the Julian Calendar was used in England, by which the year commenced with the 25th March, or the "Day of Annunciation." Upon the date mentioned (31st Dec., 1751), the Gregorian Calendar, which had long been in use on the Continent, was adopted in England, and the day after it was called the 1st Jan. 1752, by Stat. 24 George II. c. 23. But the Society of Friends, having from the first protested against using the "names of heathen gods" for the months, numbered them instead, thus calling March the 1st month, and January the 11th. A committee was appointed to consider what advice should be given to the Friends in relation to the statute in question, and the Yearly Meeting agreed to conform in omitting, after 2nd Sep. of that year, the eleven nominal days by which, owing to leap year and other causes, the New Style was in advance of the old. The Yearly Meeting also directed its Quarterly and Monthly Meetings to do the same. From the date named, therefore, Friends spoke of January as "first month," instead of March, as formerly. These documents being, with one exception, dated previous to 1752, the corresponding month of the year has been added in brackets.

CRISP'S ANSWERS TO THE DEPUTY LIEUTENANTS OF THE COUNTY OF DURHAM.

(For facsimile see p. xxiv.)

" Ye same night came ye clerke of ye deputy L^{ts.}, and examined me many questions, to wch I answered as followes :—

1. According to ye account of my parents and friends, as they have always related to me, I was borne at Colchester in Essex.

2. And I am not knowne in any country by any other name but Steven Crisp.

3. And for w^t I know I am about thirty and one or two yeares old.

4. And am by trade a weaver of serges and bays.

5. And to ye best of my remembrance I came from my outward being in ye last weeke of September.

6. And that I have a wife and two children and servants there, or had within this month.

7. And that my servants names are Henry Pomfret, Manasseh Cascetter, and John Peachy.

8. And that the last named is an apprentice.

9. And that I judge it about 200 miles thither from hence.

10. And that I came by Suffolke and Norfolke, and so thorow Lincolnshire over humber, soe downe the seacoast and into Cleavland, and over Tees, and so into this country.

11. And for great townes I came by Ipswich, thence to Norwich, thence to Linn, thence to Lincolne. Thence to hull, soe downe the seacoast into Cleavland, and over tees.

12. And that the occasion of this my travaile was only in obedience to the lord, to visit my friends that Inhabited those places.

13. And that to the best of my knowledge my travaile is at an end, and that I had beene returned before now but for awaiting this sessions."

GEORGE FOX.

(From a phototype of the painting by Sir Peter Lely.)

SYNOPSIS OF LETTERS

IN THE

CRISP COLLECTION.

1. Letter from George Fox, by George Whitehead, to Steven Crisp, without date, but in answer to one dated 4th of August [16]83.*

Friends in Holland have appealed to them for a decision as to the legality of marriage according to quaker usage. Shall they give the magistrates a copy of the certificate, or shall they invite the magistrates to be present, having given due notice of the intending ceremony? Until they hear what opinion Crisp has given, they will not write to Benjamin Furly, or any one in Holland. The case has been variously stated by Friends of Amsterdam, Friesland, and Holland; and it would have been better for them to have agreed on a course first. When Fox was there, he told them, by Benjamin Furly, that it was God's work to marry, not priests or magistrates, and he protests against the giving of money to any, whether bellman or priest.

83. Letter from George Whitehead, to Crisp, dated London, 2nd of 6th Mo. (Aug.), 1683.

B. Furly has written to R. Barclay, to be communicated to Fox and himself, concerning the giving notice of Friends marriages to the magistrates, both before and after they are consummated. Be careful not to reject this condescension, which they would look on as a great privilege, if allowed in England. Understanding that Crisp has been written to for advice, Fox and himself forbear to write to Holland until they have heard from him, and they desire to know what he has said as shortly as may be. As Furly has not insisted on the marriage taking place before the magistrates, but only notice to be given them, they wish tenderness to be shown him on account of his labours on this behalf with the Grand Pensionary. The proffer of the magistrates that Friends' marriages may be made secure, should not be let slip. For Friends have been willing from the first that their marriage should be made known

---

* See also Nos. 10, 83, and 94.

to magistrates, and published at Market Cross, as G. F. says. The
Pensionary says it should be no more to tell their intention to the
magistrates than to another man, and after, to give them a certificate
of the marriage. The trial of the widow's marriage is now at hand, it
only stops till they hear from Friends, therefore write by the next post.

2. Letter from Barclay, the Apologist, to Steven Crisp,
dated London, 3rd of 5th Mo. (July), 1676.

Some correspondence concerning the resurrection has passed between
them. He doubts not if they were together, they would quickly both
understand and accord one with another. It is a subject he never speaks
or writes about, but their importunity obliged him. He has had lately
a letter from Oldeslow, in Holstein, from the schoolmaster, one of those
Lutherans he has mentioned as interested in the writings of Wegelius,
which letter he translates below from the Latin. He has also heard
from those that have lately been with the Princess Elizabeth, that she
speaks much to Friends' advantage, and says she finds they have been
falsely reported of. After long and tedious attendance, he has nearly
finished his business, for the Duke of Lauderdale tells him yesterday
that he has received an order to give him a letter to the Council in Scotland, for the release of Friends. He purposes to be going homewards
in two or three days.

This letter, in " Collectitiæ," is wrongly attributed to John Blaykling,
which seems a strange oversight, since it bears the well-known
monogram of Barclay. The internal evidence, too, is unmistakeable,
for Blaykling was probably never out of England in his life,
while Barclay distinctly speaks of having been at Oldeslow, as well
as of the Princess Elizabeth, whom he had a few months before visited,
and was to visit again in company with Penn, the following year.
Moreover, he mentions the letter he is to deliver to the Council of Scotland as he goes homewards ; to no one in an inferior position to that of
Barclay, would the order for the release of Friends have been delivered.

The Letter from Johannes Kember, translated from the
original Latin, is copied by Barclay below. It is dated
Oldeslow, 5th of the month called July, 1676.* ("Collectitiæ,"
p. 170.)

He easily believes nothing is more acceptable to Barclay than to hear of
or see those seeking truth. Gladly would the writer meet with him and
his companion, whom he recognizes as teachers sent to draw him out of
thick darkness. He receives his brotherly admonitions with gratitude.
Is wearied of the vain delight of this world and the men of it, and

---

* There seems some discrepancy in the dates here, which even allowance for
the new style at that time adopted on the Continent, does not explain.

desires nothing more than to be hid and alone, therefore pray for him that he may not draw back.

John, the 2nd Earl of Lauderdale, succeeded to the title in 1645. He joined the Covenanters, and afterwards joined the Prince of Wales in Holland. He was taken prisoner at the battle of Worcester, and remained in confinement nine years. After the Restoration, he was made President of the Council, and Secretary of State for Scotland, until he fell under the displeasure of the Duke of York. He was created Duke of Lauderdale, 1672, which title became extinct on his death, 1682.

3. Notes of Barclay's, with references to three pages of some theological work.

4. Letter from Richard Hubberthorn, at one time a colonel in the Parliamentary Army, to Ann Blackley, wife of James Blackley, J.P., of Cambridge, all of whom joined the Society. ("Colloctitiæ," p. 30.)

Probably only a portion is here, for there is no beginning ; it proceeds to reprove for an excess of zeal, and recommends a spirit of meekness and subjection.

RICHARD HUBBERTHORN was born at Yealand, Lancashire, and was the son of a yeoman. Upon joining Friends, he left the army, and became a preacher of considerable ability. In 1654 he was imprisoned in Norwich Castle for nearly a year, for not taking off his hat before a magistrate, and for addressing a priest in the churchyard. In 1660 he went, with a letter of Fox's, to interview Charles II. They held a long discourse, which was afterwards printed, and the King promised Hubberthorn "over and again" that his friends should suffer no more for their religion, which promises, however, were speedily forgotten. The same year, he and Fox drew up a declaration setting forth their abhorrence of all plots and fighting, in order to present it to the council. This was seized when at the press ; but nothing daunted, they quickly drew up a second copy, had it printed, sent to the king and council, and distributed to the nation at large. In 1661, Hubberthorn, Burrough, and Whitehead attended the Committee of the House of Commons, and gave, at the bar, their protests and reasons against the bill which was then about to be passed, depriving Friends of the power of meeting together for worship. Their intercession was without avail ; and in April of the following year, Hubberthorn, in spite of the king's promises, was seized, violently dragged from a meeting at the Bull and Mouth, Aldgate, and taken before Alderman Richard Brown, who, after having treated him with unpardonable rudeness, committed him to Newgate. Here, owing to the crowded and insanitary state of the prison, he died after two months, June 17th, 1662.

Mrs. Blackley, although her husband was a Justice of the Peace, was imprisoned in the Tolbooth at Cambridge, for over three months, for speaking publicly against the deceit of a priest. Her husband, James Blackley, published in defence of Friends, " A Lying Wonder discovered, and the strange and terrible news from Cambridge proved false," 1659. The above letter was probably addressed to her in prison about 1656, when Hubberthorn and James Parnel were themselves sent to gaol, merely for visiting Ann Blackley in prison.

5. An account of a case tried at Nottingham Assizes, respecting some property, dated Nottingham, 8th of 6th Mo. (Aug.), 1661.

5A. A copy of the same.

6. Letter from Katherine Evans, dated Wo[rce]ster, 14th of 3rd Mo. (May), 1672, to Steven Crisp. (" Collectitiæ," p. 167.)

Gladly would the writer have seen his face at Worcester, but hopes to do so at Bristol in fair time. Her companion, Mary Gainer, desires her love. She rejoices over the prosperity of Sion in England, Ireland, and other countries.

KATHERINE EVANS was the wife of John Evans, of Inglishcombe, near Bath, a man of considerable property, who was several times imprisoned in his own county, for preaching, and who finally died in prison, 14th of January, 1664. The same year, Mrs. Evans was arrested for preaching in the market-place at Salisbury, beaten, and sent out of the city. She returned the next month, and was then imprisoned. In 1658, with Sarah Cheevers, Katherine Evans sailed for Leghorn, intending to proceed to Alexandria. They were landed at Malta, and here underwent a painful imprisonment by the Inquisition, lasting for four years.

After her return to England, she was several times in prison, and lived to a great age, dying in 1692.

7. Letter from James Parnel to Steven Crisp. Without date ; found in 1764. (Callaway's Memoir of James Parnel, London, 1846, p. 71.)

Encourages him not to be weary of the yoke, and not to be hasty to know anything, for thus Eve lost her Paradise.

JAMES PARNEL, whose name has ever been held in memory and respect, as the first of the Quakers who suffered death for his opinions, was born at Retford, near Nottingham, about 1636. He was one of those children, not uncommon, who, to a somewhat imperfect physical organization, unite prematurely developed mental gifts. He was short and insignificant in person, and was therefore called in ridicule, "The quaking boy." There is little information about his early life, only that he was, as Sewel puts it, "trained up in the schools of literature," which means probably that he went to the grammar school in Retford. Judging from the tact and ability afterwards displayed in routing his antagonists, and scattering their arguments, he must have made excellent use of the time spent in study. What he was doing in Carlisle, I cannot tell, but he says he had heard of a "seeking people," and doubtless he set out to find them. In 1652, when Fox was lying in the dungeon there, committed by Wilfrey Lawson the High Sheriff, the lad, drawn perhaps out of curiosity, went to see this notorious preacher, and disturber of the peace. Fox, as his habit was, began to expound his Quakerism, and the young Parnel was so "effectually reached," that he at once began both to preach and to write his new opinions. In 1654 he published, "A Trial of Faith, etc.," which was several times reprinted, and translated into Dutch, French, and German. The same year he was imprisoned in Cambridge by William Pickering, the Mayor, for publishing papers against the corruption of magistrates and priests. He laid there two sessions. In March, 1655, he was at Fenstanton, in Huntingdonshire, preaching, when a number of the Baptists, under Richard Elligood their teacher, engaged him in dispute, and he drew up forty-three queries to be read in their congregation. The next month, he was engaging in a public argument at Cambridge with one Hind, a tanner, and John Doughty. Being disappointed of the place the Baptists had promised, the meeting took place first in Hind's house, then in his yard, where, finally, a great number of undergraduates, of whom Fox says that "the miners, colliers, and carters could not be ruder," and others, collected and made a violent uproar. In the end, Parnell was arrested for causing a tumult. In May, he was at Littleport, in the Isle of Ely, preaching in a Friend's orchard, when John Ray, of Wickombruck, Suffolk, a Baptist teacher, came to denounce Samuel and Ezekiel Cater, who had formerly been elders among the Baptists. Parnell engaged in spiritual warfare with Ray at some length, as related by him in "The Watcher, etc.," 1655, 4to. Samuel Cater was, as he says in the *Testimony* prefixed to Parnel's *Works*, 1675, 4to, "turned unto the truth" by Parnel, and was "constrained by the great love he bore him, to be his constant companion in his daily preachings and wanderings," concerning which therefore he speaks with some authority, that they were performed in "gravity, humility, and blameless conversation." At Midsummer, 1655, James Parnel passed into Essex, and after having preached at Felsted, Stebbing, Witham, Coggeshall, Halstead and other places, he arrived at Colchester one Saturday, and on the following day, "preached the gospel to many thousands of people." (Crisp's *Testimony*.) Early in the morning he must have begun preaching in his lodging, then, when service was over in the churches, he was allowed to speak in one of them, probably St. Nicholas. In the afternoon, or evening, he engaged in a public dispute with the Town Lecturer, or preacher, viz., chaplain to the Mayor, an office now abolished, the last being Dr. John Edwards, appointed in 1700 (see Morant). All this formed a long day's work for a young preacher of only eighteen or nineteen, but the whole of that week was spent in similar labours. Then, hearing of a public fast appointed for the 12th July, 1655, at Coggeshall, specially to pray against the errors of the quakers, he at once repaired thither "to defend the truth." When Priest Willis, of Braintree, had ended his discourse in the parish church of St. Peter's, Coggeshall, young Parnel arose and commenced to address the congregation, but confusion ensued, and he, accompanied by numerous of his friends and supporters, left the building. Justice Wakering followed, and arrested him in the name of the Protector, suffering, however, a Friend to engage himself as surety for Parnel's return, as soon as the hour of worship after their own manner, to which they were now bound, was over.

The same afternoon, or the following morning, Parnell was brought before four justices, viz. :—Herbert Pelham, Thomas Cook, Dionysius Wakering, and William Harlackenden, with whom were many priests, Sparrow of Halstead, Stalham of Terling, Samms of Coggeshall, and others not named. The array of persons who here sat in judgment on Parnel brings forcibly before us the fact that the real opponents of the early Friends were the Puritans. Up to the time of Fox, the religious teaching of the country had been in their hands. It was not, therefore, quakerism fighting against irreligion, so much as against a calvinistic puritanism in deadly earnest. If we enquire into the history of these priests, we find that they were all three, William Sparrow,

John Stalham, and John Samms, steadfast Nonconformists, ejected from their livings by the Act of Uniformity, in 1662, and who then founded Congregational churches.   They were all three, as well as Dionysius Wakering, on Cromwell's Commission for the 'trying' of suitable ministers.   The latter sate for Essex, in Cromwell's first parliament, 3rd Sep., 1654–22nd Jan., 1655.   Stalham wrote a book against the Quakers called "The Reviler Rebuked," London, 1657, dedicated to "His Highness Oliver, Lord Protector of the Commonwealth, and the Right Honourable the Council of State."   It was in answer to Richard Farnworth (see Davids' "Annals of Evangelical Nonconformity in Essex, 1863, Part II., Memorials ").

After the justices had heard the case, Parnel was committed to the common gaol at Colchester.   Here he remained until the assizes, which, being held at Chelmsford, the unfortunate youth, by this time much weakened physically by incessant preaching, and prison life, was compelled to tramp the long eighteen miles on the highway, chained to common murderers and felons.   His trial took place before Judge Hills, and, although the jury found him innocent of everything except of writing a reply to his mittimus, and of having no settled habitation, the judge imposed a fine of £40 upon him, and returned him to prison.   While here, he wrote "Goliah's head cut off with his own sword, &c., in reply to a book by an unnamed author, whom I understand to be one Thomas Draton, a teacher at Abbey Rippon, Huntingdonshire," 1655, 4to; "The Fruits of a Fast," 1655, 4to, which contains a full relation of his arrest, trial, and imprisonment ; and many "Epistles" to his friends in Essex, London, and elsewhere.   His imprisonment lasted about ten or eleven months, and was endured under circumstances of extreme hardship, too well-known to be repeated in detail here.   A full account will be found in Sewel's "History of the Rise," &c., Vol. I., pp. 137—141. Suffice it to say, that the damp, unlit hole in the massive walls of the Castle, about the size of a baker's oven, which formed his cell, and from which he had to climb twelve feet, or more, to an opening, to fetch his victuals, has ever since formed an object of interest to numbers of visitors to Colchester, both English and American.   At twenty years old, this young quaker, after five years' incessant preaching, disputing, and travelling on foot to visit numbers of outlying villages, died in this miserable cell, and it is no wonder that he became at once exalted into a hero, and regarded as divinely inspired, since his polemical spirit, and his ability in argument, added to his pure life, and native eloquence, gave him a wider notoriety than that of many a more ripe and seasoned quaker. Ann Langley, several times mentioned in these letters, was with him when he died, and brought Sewel, the historian, to the place not long after, relating as an eye-witness, all the painful story. Parnel's body was not allowed to be claimed by his friends, but was buried in the Castle-yard.

8. A letter from George Whitehead to Crisp, dated London, 30th of 1st Mo. (March), 1672.

Before Crisp's letter came to hand, he had drawn up a similar paper, which Thomas Moore had given to the king, with a list of those under prœmunire, etc. This hath hitherto been effectual, in order to a further inquiry. How far the king and council have proceeded, he leaves it to William Crouch to inform him. His paper is kept for another occasion, if need be, but they are encouraged to hope well, for divers reasons. The council yesterday signed the letters to the sheriffs, so they will be shortly received in the counties.

On the other side is the copy of a circular addressed to the sheriffs of the counties, requiring them to return to the council, lists of Friends confined in their respective gaols, dated Whitehall,—of March, 1672.

Also a letter signed by George Whitehead, Gerard Roberts, Thomas Moore, John Osgood, William Welsh, and Ellis Hookes, to Friends of Colchester.

Upon the king's suspension of the penal laws in matters ecclesiastical, they were encouraged to hope that all Friends, under whatever sentence, should be released. Thomas Moore waited upon him, and procured the above order. Some important Friends should apply to the sheriff, and see that he make a favourable return. He need not mention the original offence. The payment of tithes is expected in the king's declaration, so they do not expect the release of those committed by priests under common law writ. The sufferings of Friends are much upon them, and the writers do not question their care in the matter, but rather could not omit this weighty concern on their behalf.

ELLIS HOOKES was for twenty-four years the Recording Clerk of the Society. All matters relating to the members of the different meetings passed through his hands, and his letters contained in the Swarthmore MSS. and other collections, are full of interest, containing all the current news from London. He wrote "Dedicatory Epistles," as the custom of the day was, to the works of Fisher, Burrough, Smith, Howgill, Parnel, &c., and published, with Fox, "A Primer and Catechism for Children," 1670, and "An Instruction for Right Spelling," 1673, besides some religious books. He died of consumption, 12th September, 1681.

WILLIAM CROUCH was born at Penton-by-Wayhill, a small village near Andover, Hampshire, on the 5th April, 1628. His father was a substantial yeoman, and his mother a strict Puritan, so that he received a religious training. The early death of his father, cut William's education short, and he was sent as an apprentice to London, where he eventually rose to a position of substantial repute and means, as an upholsterer. Being chosen as a public officer in Broad Street Ward of the City, and declining to take the oath, or to pay what was called " garnish money," he was imprisoned in a " small hole among common prisoners," until discharged upon application to John Frederic, the Lord Mayor. Three months after, at the suit of Samuel Clark, vicar of St. Bennet Fink, he was lodged in the Poultry Compter, for one year and three quarters, for non-payment of tithes. On the 23rd of Ausust, 1665, he was, with seven other Friends, arrested at Peel Meeting, and committed to the Gatehouse at Westminster, under an order from the Duke of Albemarle. The plague was raging at the time, and the prison vilely infected, so that prisoners were dying four or five in a night. During his imprisonment, Crouch exchanged letters and epistles with William Wickens, the chaplain of the gaol, on oaths and other subjects, as well as with Clark, the vicar.

Crouch's house in Finch Lane was burned during the great fire, and on the rebuilding of the city, he settled in Crown Court, Gracechurch Street. He was immediately called to pay tithes to the Rev. John Cliff, rector of St. Bennet's, which refusing, his goods were seized. He was also distrained upon under the Conventicle Act in 1683, for being present at a meeting in White Hart Court, on the 13th of June, and again under a warrant from Thomas Jenner, Recorder of London, in 1684.

Crouch married Ruth Brown, who died a few months before himself. His own death took place, at the age of eighty-two, on the 13th of January, 1710. (" Posthuma Christiana," edited, with some account of the writer, William Crouch, by Richard Claridge, London, 1712.)

9. Edward Riggs' letter and draft of his will. No date.

" DEAR FRIEND S. C.,—My dear love most heartily remembered to thee, and I should be heartily glad that I might once more see thee, but whether ever I shall, the Lord only knoweth. I am at this time, and hath been a great while, very infirm of body, and full of trouble and pain, insomuch that I verily think my time cannot be long in this world ; and I could have willingly advised with thee concerning the disposal of that little portion God hath lent me, and which I have now left in this world, but I must now be content without it.

I troubled thee with such business some years ago, (viz.) soon after my wife died, and that will thou made for me I have now by me, but since that, there is a great alteration in my estate, and also some in my family, which necessitate me to make a new will ; for though I have (I think) been careful and a good husband, yet (though it be with shame), I must need tell thee one of my housen I gave to my younger daughter, is mortgaged, and I still owe a great deal of money [to] my friends even with the necessaries and things considerable I left to my son. One of my elder daughters is dead, and the other married. My disbursements for her, and my son, I have as near as I can computed, with what goods that I know they have, and what I do not know I must let pass ; so that now things being as they are, my three youngest children will have but little, yet I am willing they should have all I leave, and I think with good reason ; for I would willingly discharge my conscience and die at peace, for when I think of their dear mother, my loving, careful, and painful wife, it makes me heartily sorry I have no more to leave them, of what she was so industrious for, thinking it for their good.

Therefore I do desire that thou would once more take the trouble upon thee for me (and I hope for their good), to draw up my will, in such sound form as may exclude all pretended legal claimants, or heirs to what I leave, for I know I shall not please my two elder children, but I can't now help it. My design is to preserve my own peace. My will, in as good order as I can express it, I will here give thee in rough draft; as short, as full, as plain and simple, as my mind and thought can deliver it, designing thee to methodize it, as thou so canst.

First, then, my will is, that my debts be computed with the money upon the mortgage, also, and likewise, my personal estate what and wherefore it be money, debts or goods ; and that my executors sell the farm and pay my debts, and summon all charges as far as they will extend.

And as in my former will, I give unto my daughter, Anna Riggs, and my daughter Sarah Riggs, all that my copyhold tenement in Woodbridge, called the Greyhound, now in the occupation of Henry Pessy, or his assignees, holders of the Manor of Woodbridge, Rasleton, by equal moyeties and half-parts, (viz.) : to Ann and her heirs for ever, the one part ; and Sarah and her heirs for ever, the other part. And then, as in my last, I give and bequeath unto my daughter, Elizabeth Riggs, and her heirs for ever, my two small tenements adjoining to the Greyhound, in the occupation of Richard Horne, and William Fuller, or their assignees, holden of the manor aforesaid, with this proviso, that if either of them die before they come to the proper possession thereof, that then the whole estate be equally divided between the survivors, either a like part.

Then I give unto my son Thomas Riggs, and to my daughter Mary, now the wife of William Norton, each the sum of twenty shillings, to be paid within a year and one day, after my decease, and of which, and all my remaining debts, my will is that, after my executors have taken up the housen for my three daughters aforesaid, that they receive the rents and profits thereof, until they have discharged all my debts, and closed the mortgage, and legacies, and paid themselves their proper costs, both trouble and charge concerning this my will. And also may, if they please and see convenient, give my son Thomas the sum of five pound more, beside what is before expressed (that is, when my debts are discharged), out of the rents and profits of my housen aforesaid ; and when all is discharged, paid, and done, to return them to my daughters aforesaid, if they be capable, otherwise to take care of them, and for them till they be.

And I make my trusty friends John Lawrence, of Bouly, and Thomas Linde, Rendlesham, my executors, and my brother-in-law, Clement Carter, of Woodbridge, super-adviser ; and further, my will is that, if either of my children shall object, disallow, or not be content with the doings and orders of this my three trusty friends, or to the survivor, or survivors, if either or any of them chance to die, that then to accept of ten shillings for their part, and be utterly excluded.

So, dear friend, having given thee the sum of my mind, I desire thee to form the same as speedily, and send me it as presently, as thou canst ; for I rest unsatisfied till I see it accomplished.

I rest as deeply obliged, thy truly loving Friend,

EDWARD RIGGS."

112.   Letter from Clement Carter to Crisp, from Melton Gaol, 21st of 10th Mo. (Dec.), [16]85, concerning the will of Edward Rigg, see No. 9.

His, and fellow prisoners', love to Crisp and his wife. Has had some debate about the substance of E. Riggs will, with the executors, Thos. Linde being chief actor, because Jo. Lawrence is in prison. Many unexpected claims have come to light, debts come in but slowly, so that he is pent for money. He has taken up the Grey-hound which is to come to the two eldest girls, but not the two tenements, upon which there is a mortgage of £40. Unless he can have the £10 in Crisp's hands, and the £10 in Eliz. Bennets towards the redemption, he will let it fall. Jo. Lawrence and himself conceive it will be best so to do, else Edwards will is not carried out, and the younger girls will be hardly dealt with to pay £40, and, as it were, a double fine. It will be a long time before the houses, at £6 per annum, will pay the mortgage interest, taxations, and fine. If now redeemed, part will be saved. Edward spoke to him of the money in their hands, and allotted it in his mind to the use now spoken of.

He has enclosed the very letter written to Crisp, some time before Edward died, desiring him to draw up his will by those directions. But Crisp was at Yearly Meeting, and from thence went on to Holland, before the letter could be got to him, so the writer drew up Edward's will at his desire, in the form directed in this letter. Would have sent a copy of the will *verbatim*, but had none ready. Desires answer to be sent by Solomon Freemantel, or his kinsman, next second-day, for they expect a court soon, and if they be assured of that money, they will take [the mortgage] up. Friends in prison were in debate about it this day, and decided it would be prejudicial to let it fall. Elizabeth Bennet is a prisoner, and waits an answer to this. Peter Cross, John Lawrence, and all Friends send love. Two courts are already past. The time is now at hand to take it up or let it fall.

10, 57, and 93.   Letters from Benjamin Furly, dated from Rotterdam, 3rd of 8th Mo. (Oct.), 1683 ; 17th of 7th Mo. (Sept.), 1683 ; and 2nd of 8th Mo. (Oct.), 1683 ; the two first to Crisp, the last to George Lawrie.

All relating to the legal solemnisation of quaker marriages in Holland. Due notice shall be given of the intention to the magistrates, for the preservation of law and order in the State. In the first letter, he tells how he has been to the Hague, waiting upon the Pensionery for an audience. Excitement prevails, owing to the order given for the arrest of the D[uke] of M[onmouth], should he appear. The Spanish and Brandenburg envoys came in, and again hindered him. The second letter raises a point of variance between Crisp and Furly, still in relation to the marriage question. The third letter is forwarded to Crisp, and endorsed by George Whitehead. It accompanied one to Barclay, and is to be shown to Fox. (See also Nos. 1, 83, and 94).

BENJAMIN FURLY was born at Colchester, on the 13th of April, 1636, and began life as a merchant there, early joining the Friends. Previous to 1677 he went to live at Rotterdam, for in that year George Fox stayed at his house, and Furly acted as interpreter for his tour in Holland and Germany. He also travelled with Penn. His house became the rendezvous of Leclerc, Limborch, and other learned men, and he entertained Algernon Sydney, Locke, and the third Lord Shaftesbury. He corresponded with Sydney and Locke, and wrote various works, beside translating others from Dutch into English. He died in 1714. The catalogue of his valuable library, sold after his death, was published. A fourth paper of Furly's appears as No. 104 in this Collection. It is a copy, dated Rotterdam, 1669, of his recantation of certain papers given forth by him respecting the wearing of the hat in prayer. The Furlys were a numerous family in Colchester. Furly's father, John Furly, was Mayor of Colchester, 1650 and 1652. (Cromwell's " History of Colchester," pp. 397-8).

11 and 20. Jacob Telner's answer to George Keith's doctrine in his Catechism.

The life of GEORGE KEITH presents an extraordinary history of religious enthusiasm, unregulated by settled convictions. He was born about 1639, near Aberdeen, and became a Scholar and M.A. of Marischal College, Aberdeen. He was designed for the Presbyterian ministry, but in 1662 joined the quakers, being first convinced by William Dewsbury. In 1664 he was imprisoned for ten months in Aberdeen. Keith rendered considerable assistance to the Apologist in his great work, and also wrote with Barclay two treatises, " Quakerism no Popery," and " Quakerism Confirmed." He emigrated to America in 1689, and upon the deaths of Fox and Penn soon after, he relinquished some of the quaker tenets. A controversy ensued, Keith and his followers calling themselves " Christian quakers," and established a " consolatory repast from house to house," i.e., a form of the Lord's supper. His dispute with the Philadelphian Quakers caused Keith to be disowned by London

Yearly Meeting, whom he on his part also disowned. He set up a meeting at Turner's Hall, and continued preaching against the Friends, retaining their garb and speech, and administering baptism and the supper. In 1702 he returned to America, as one of the first missionaries sent out by the Society for the Propagation of the Gospel, and was eminently successful. Returning to England in 1704, he became lecturer at Allhallows, Lombard Street, and was soon after presented by Archbishop Tenison to the living of Edburton, Sussex, where he died on 27th March, 1716.

20. Crisp to Jacob Telner ; no date.

He has always taken notice that his progress in the truth is harder by reason of his natural temper, which is mixed with zeal to get forward, and attain to high things. Hopes to hear of Telners daughter, who must now be come to years of discretion. If she follow the light in her own conscience, she will be a comfort to her parents, and lovely to all her friends.

12. Letter from Deborah Roelofs to Crisp, dated Hamburg, 2nd of 8th Mo. (Oct.), 1670.

She and her husband both desire that love may have its free passage, without hindrance because of things of less worth. [The letter is in English, but the writer is evidently more at home in her native Dutch.]

41. Letter from Jan Roelofs, husband of the preceding ; no date ; partly in Dutch.

After his dear wife had written, and let him read the enclosed, he was moved in his heart to write a few words. . . . . Wishes to greet E. H[endricks], J. Jacops, Isaac Jacops, his good brother, Gertrude, and Elizabeth Cr[is]p, [he means probably Crisp's wife Dorothy, as his mother Elizabeth was dead. Adds a p.s.] But just now has received through Stijnter, a deal of books, to be perused, which having done, he finds them to be in that spirit of keeping on the hat in prayer. Intends to burn them in the fire. Stijnter feels Crisp's words to her to be sound and good. He may expect a letter from her.

The above alludes to a certain schism, introduced by John Perrot, about keeping the hat on in prayer. Some verses written *In Memoriam*, by Martin Mason, are to be found on the back of the title page of " John Perrot's Vision," and in a letter to a friend, (Mason MSS., Devonshire House) the latter says, pertinently, " What matter whether hat be on or off, as long as heart be right." Perrot was at one time of his life of somewhat doubtful sanity, and was imprisoned for a period in an asylum at Rome, whither he had gone on a mission to convert the Pope. He travelled extensively in Greece, Italy, America, and Barbadoes, and finally died in Jamaica, about 1682.

13.   An address to the inhabitants of London, cautioning against the sin of pride, by George Whitehead, dated 18th of 7th Mo. (Sept.), 1693.

A printed Broadside.

14.   Letter from Crisp to Jonathan Haddock, dated London, 8th of 11th Mo., 1673.   (Jan., 1674).

Has heard that Haddock went to R. Clark's to witness against the proceedings of Friends against the rioters.   It was not wisely done, for it gives evidence of division.   It is right to lay grievances before the magistrates, else they are no friends to justice.   An order is given that all sufferings through not opening shops on a certain day [Christmas day], be sent to London.

15.   Journal, in his own handwriting, of Crisp's travel into the West of England ; diurnal, from 27th of 8th Mo. (Oct.) to 11th of 11th Mo., 1669 (Jan., 1670).   See Introduction.

16 and 100.   Two letters from Mrs. E. Bradford to Crisp, dated Arksey (West Rid., Yorks.), 24th of 1st Mo. (March), and 6th of 2nd Mo. (April), 16—.

1. She hath not forgotten him, though prevented by illness from writing.   A prison cannot shut him out from the flowing of her love. *2.* She received his, dated 29th of 9th Mo., and rejoices he is free again.   Many about Thorne, Hatfield, and Fishlake are prisoners at York.   Since the new Sheriff took possession of the castle, some have been liberated.

17.   Preface of a Dutch translation of some English work, " The Translator to the Reader," Rotterdam.

18, 47, 62, 65, 95, 99, and 128.   Letters from Peter Hendricks, of Amsterdam, to Crisp, and others, relating chiefly to money affairs of Friends in Holland.

128.   " A Testimony of the Love of God and of the Faith of Abraham," written in English, and signed Peter Hendricks, Amsterdam, 4th of 1st Mo. (March), 1667.   (" Collectitiæ," p. 144.)

99.   Letter to Gertrude Dericks (G.D.N.), in Dutch, dated Amsterdam, 26th of 9th Mo. (Nov.), 1677, and enclosing a bill, in English, to William Crouch, for buttons supplied, amounting to the sum of 209fl. 4st. ; and to John Vander Wall, of Harwich, for Four Maps of the world, and charges to Rotterdam, amounting to 15fl. 16st.   It appears that

Hendricks and Claus [see below] had a business partnership.

62. Letter to Franciscus M. van Helmont, in Dutch, dated Amsterdam, 24th of 12th Mo., 1681 (Feb.), 1682.

95. Letter to Crisp, in Dutch, dated Amsterdam, 3rd of 8th Mo. (Oct.), 1683.

65. Paper dated Amsterdam, 11th July, 1688, signed by Peter Hendricks, B. v. Tongere, Jan. Claus, Peter Roelofs, Jacob Claus, and Pieter Heus, on behalf of the Two Weeks' meeting at Amsterdam, concerning the sum of £364 sterling, set apart by Gertrude Dericks Nieson, for the service of the truth and the furthering of the gospel, for which the above named remain surety, the interest to be paid twice yearly by them on the 24th of July and December.

On the other side, a letter to Crisp, dated Amsterdam, 13th Sept., 1688.

18. Letter to Crisp, in Dutch, Amsterdam, 23rd of 6th Mo. (Aug.), 1692.

19, 27, 28, 75, 131, 132. Letters from Jan Claus, to Crisp, and others.

27. Claus to Crisp, in Dutch, no date, but in answer to one of 9th *December*, [16] 71, which points to its being written in 1672, and before the writer became a Friend. He recounts his history, and study of the writings of Tauler, Wegelius, Sebastian Franken, and Jacob Böhme, and other German Mystics of the 16th and 17th centuries.

19. Letter from Hilary Prache to Claus, copied by the latter. Oldebergh, 3rd of 3rd Mo. (May), 1673.

Claus' letter of the 7th of the 2nd Mo. (April) he received on the 28th of the same, in Breslau, likewise those from E. H. [Elizabeth Hendricks, see No. 70], and (as he supposes) her husband P. H., which were pleasant to him. His name is Hilarius Prache, which in Holland and England is well-known to Professors of the Hebrew tongue, as the translator of a treatise by Jedaia Happenini, a Spanish Jew, called *Bakkascha, sive meditatio, cujus singulæ voces à Mem incipiunt, pactis vocalibus adornata, Latine explicata, notis & illustrata opera et studio Hilary Prachy, Ligio Silesi.* Impress, Lipsæ, Anno 1662, in 4to. He came to Oldeburgh from Liegnitz, eleven miles from Breslau, where he was pastor and senior from 1662 to 1669. From Hamburgh, or Berlin, to Breslau is eighty-six miles. The catalogue desired by Claus of the books he already has, is nearly finished. Of English books, he has only the Bible, an English grammar by John Wallis, printed in Hamburg the preceding year, "The Pearl found in England," and "To the Turk and all under his Supream [Rule]," by G.F. [George Fox]. Half-a-mile from thence, in five villages, right in the middle of the Lutherans, live a people called Svenkfelden, who have learned the truth differently from others, who remain still when others bow, sing, and read the Picardier hymns, have continued thereabouts for 150 years, and are not unlike the Mennonists. They are sore pressed by the new magistrate. They believe in infant baptism, attend neither Lutheran, or Papist Churches, and (they say) have lived twelve years without being molested by either Lutheran or Papist magistrates. They frequent his house, for he, when a student, at college, for three years, had met with a similar Consistory near Liegnitz, calling themselves Collegianten. He has had the works of G. K. [George Keith] and the like, fifty-five books. Has also corresponded with Elizabeth Hendricks, whose letters he finds full of teaching.

HILARIUS PRACHE was born in 1614 at Teutschel, near Liegnitz, being the son of the pastor of that place. His early days were spent in Breslau, and in Hungary, whence he returned poor and unsatisfied, with a decided inclination towards mysticism, and having become an acknowledged Hebrew scholar. After teaching in noble families for some time, he was ordained in Breslau, 1651, and appointed pastor of Diersdorf. He is chiefly known as the learned translator of "Bakkascha," a Hebrew treatise by a Spanish rabbi named Jedaia Happenini, which work he alludes to in the above letter. His leaning towards mysticism becoming more pronounced, he was compelled to resign his office, and in 1674 he left Germany for London, where he and his family sought out and joined the quakers. He was afterwards employed for some time as a corrector and translator in the printing press at Cambridge. He died in 1679.

The COLLEGIANTEN were a body of Christians closely connected with the Waterlander Mennonites (see No. 36), although holding that the office of teacher had ceased in the church, who "needed not that any man should teach them," because the bible now exists, &c. Preaching they held should be open to all spiritually minded Christians. On the introduction of more liberal and enlightened views among the Mennonites, the Collegianten lost their *raison d'être*. Their last General Assembly was held in 1787 at Ruuysberg, and in 1791 their meetings at Amsterdam and Rotterdam ceased.

CASPAR SCHWENKSFELD, who is termed by Dr. Dorner in his "History of Protestant Theology," the noblest representative of the theoretical mysticism of the age of the Reformation, was a Silesian nobleman, born in 1490. On attaining his majority, he joined the Court of Duke Charles of Munsterberg, and afterwards lived for many years with Duke Frederick of Liegnitz. At Munsterburg he learned of John Huss, and commenced to study Tauler. Luther's conduct at Worms completed the conviction that his religion hitherto had not been of the heart. He retired to private

life, and studied the Scriptures "day and night." Upon conferring with
Luther at Wittenberg, a grave divergence in their views became evident.
Schwenksfeld held that the Reformation should proceed from within outwardly, and not from without inwardly. He disapproved of linking the
Reformed Church with the State, and said the Lutherans were forming
a church by power and command of the magistrate, not gathering one
first formed by Christ's spirit. Schwenksfeld's teaching was in complete
accordance with George Fox's on three cardinal points : inward light,
immediate revelation, and the denying of bodily acts, such as the
sacraments, to maintain spiritual life. Schwenksfeld underwent much
persecution from the clergy, who maintained that he, as a layman, had
no right to teach. He was banished from Liegnitz, forbidden to exercise
his religion, and finally excommunicated by Luther. Worn out in body
and mind, he died at Ulm, 10th December, 1561. His followers were
persecuted, imprisoned, and banished, especially between 1719 and 1734,
when a body of them emigrated to England, and finally settled in Pennsylvania, where they still maintain their existence as a distinct religious
sect. His history is eminently interesting, and will amply repay further
study.

19. On the back is a letter from Claus to Crisp, Gertrude
(Dericks) and Lysbet (Hendricks) dated Amsterdam, the 28th
of 3rd Mo. (May), 1673.

He received yesterday Hilary Prache's letter, of which he has made a
Dutch copy on the other side. Read it attentively. The writer [of it]
heard the preaching of William Ames in Breslau. Greet him affection-
ately to Th. Gr., W. Penn, Jam. Parke, W. Welch, W. Crouch, John
Furly, Ezek. Woolley and Mary, Dorothy Crisp, John Casimir, and other
Friends.

In Rep. II. of the Hist. MSS., App. vi., p. 16, Ezekiel Woolley, of
Spitalfields, is mentioned as attending a Meeting House at Plaistow, 1676.

28. The same to G.D.N., in Dutch, with postscript in
English ; Amsterdam, 18th of 9th Mo. (Nov.), 1677.

This letter, like No. 99, is addressed to Gertrude Dericks, afterwards
Crisp (called by Fox in his Journal, Gertrude Dericks Niesen), while she
is on a visit to Steven and Dorothy Crisp, at Colchester, having returned
from Holland with Penn and Fox, in October, 1677.

His esteem is great for her, in that for the service of truth she has
offered herself [to visit England]. He will open his heart as a child,
and the more so as she has S.C. near by, that they together may advise
him. He has desired that life and power may spread through all the
earth, but sees not the way, only desires to help. In his last journey
with William Penn to Germany [as interpreter], his mouth was a little
opened, but since his return, things have not been well. Has felt

something arising in his heart to say in the meeting, but was surrounded with reasonings and fears, till he has wished himself somewhere in a corner, that with tears and weeping he might ease himself. Can they give him a word of counsel that the cloud shall quickly vanish. His love is to her dear children, and Dorothy Crisp, Solomon and Sarah Freemantel, Mary Bray, and George Weatherley.

131. **The same to Friends of London Yearly Meeting, in English, Amsterdam, ₇₆ of ⅓ Mo., 1686 (6th May).**

He is asked by the quarterly meeting at Amsterdam, to inform Friends in London of the state of affairs on the Continent. In Amsterdam, Rotterdam, Haarlem, Alkmaar, and in Friesland, the meetings are peaceable and well; also at Embden, Frederickstatt, and Hamburg, since the ending of their troubles (by the assistance of S. C[risp]) the year before. In Dantzic there is trouble, through disturbers of their peace falsely reporting them to the Burgomaster. The meetings in the Palatinate, and at Crefeld, are dissolved by the emigration of all their members to Pennsylvania. The fund for those who suffer for the truth is now reduced to £16. 5s. If Friends in Dantzic are involved, as they fear, in greater trouble, prison, and so forth, they will need help, since they cannot continue their trades.

75. **The same to Crisp, in Dutch, Amsterdam, 3rd of 10th Mo. (Dec.), 1687.**

132. **The same to John Furly, of Colchester, in English, dated Amsterdam, ₁₁ of ₁₂ Mo., 1693 (1st Dec.).**

He duly received the books forwarded soon after Furly's return to England. Concerning Crisp's books, brother J. Roelofs says he sent a catalogue long ago; they have no copy of it, and to make another would cost much time. Steven wrote nothing in Dutch, but always first in English. He kept all his MSS. himself, and he believes many that have not been printed will be found among his papers. He will make another catalogue, if wished; and will be glad to open a correspondence as to the welfare of Friends in Holland. Jacob Telner is with them, and salutes all in Colchester. He wishes love to Furly's wife, and all his relations; his wife, Peter Hendricks and his wife desire the same. Particularly salutes his brother, Benjamin Furly, and his wife, hopes she and the little one are well, and looks for an order for buttons from his brother.

JAN CLAUS was a merchant of Amsterdam, who settled in England, where he joined the Society. His brother Jacob Claus, was a printer and bookseller in Amsterdam. In 1664, being in London, he was arrested, tried at the Old Bailey, and in spite of his plea that he was a foreigner, sentenced to transportation for seven years to Jamaica. With fifty-five others, he sailed on the 20th of July, in the *Black Spread Eagle*. Many on board died of the plague and close confinement; but Claus lived to return to Holland, and continue his work. He married a sister of Dr. Hasbert, of Embden, but never returned to London. He acted as interpreter to Fox on his visit to Holland and Germany in 1677. (Crouch's "Posthuma Christiana," 1712, p. 89.)

21. George Fox, junior, to Crisp, dated Lambeth House, 16th of 5th Mo. (July), 1660. ("Collectitiæ," p. 20.)

Immortal power only can preserve them in the day of trial. Fears some may be hurt by flattery, and others by reason of desperate cruelty. Meetings in London are pretty quiet, so far as he knows. His fellow-prisoner and himself have leave from the gaoler to walk in the garden sometimes.

GEORGE FOX, JUNIOR, was no relation to the founder of the Society. Although an older man, he took the title of junior, because he said he had not witnessed the second birth until long after his namesake. For preaching at a meeting at Harwich, Fox, with Gressingham, an admiralty shipwright, who was convinced, and voluntarily accompanied him, was sent by order of Parliament, on the representation of the Mayor of Harwich, to Lambeth Gate House, and kept there week after week, no notice being taken of their case. While in prison at Harwich, he wrote "A Noble Salutation of Charles Stuart," dated 16th May, 1660, in which he reviewed the affairs of the nation for many years, pointed out to the King wherein his father's government had committed evil, and brought punishment upon themselves, "although I shall not say but that some of them went beyond their commission against thy father when they were brought as a rod over you." He warned the King not to countenance pride or oppression, nor to seek revenge on his former enemies. He also wrote, in Lambeth prison, "England's Sad Estate and Condition Lamented," pub. Lond., 1661, and "The Dread of God's Power uttering His voice through man unto the heads of the nation," dated 28th July, 1660. He died at Hurst, Sussex, 7th July, 1661.

22. The Princess Elizabeth of the Palatine, to Crisp.

Ye 2 of May. [1672.]

"Yor good wishes for our family, and intentions to come and see me are very acceptable. What could not be performed this tyme, may be in another season. in ye meanwhile I shall indeavor to practis yor lesons, as God shall aford me strength. I have bin out of my native contry above seventeen yeares, and know not what passed ther. if my brother did refuse protection unto Godly persons, it is ill for him, but the better for them, to have noe share in ye desolation of yt poor ruined contry. God will gather all yt live in obedience to him wher and when he pleases. I recomend to yor prayers one yt loves all yt love ye Lord Jesus Christ, named yor unknown friend in Him.

ELIZABETH."

ELIZABETH, Princess Palatine, and Abbess of Herwerden, or Herford, in Westphalia, without doubt one of the most talented women of her own, or any other time, was the eldest daughter, and third child, of

Elizabeth Stuart, daughter of James I., and Frederick V., King of Bohemia. She was born at Heidelberg, on the 10th November, 1618, and when about a year old, the youthful couple, her parents, whose marriage in London had been celebrated with such extraordinary pomp and splendour, were lured into accepting the dazzling positions of King and Queen of Bohemia. Before twelve months had passed, however, their dream of regal state had vanished. Frederick was exhorted, by the Emperor of Austria, to surrender his crown within a month, on pain of excommunication. The Palatinate was invaded by a hostile army under the Marquis Spinola, and "The Winter King" and his young wife fled, in peril of their lives, to the Hague, where the remainder of the Queen's life was spent.

Elizabeth's early childhood was passed under the guardianship of her grandmother, the Electress Louise Juliana, daughter of William the Silent. She was a woman of strongly marked character, well balanced, upright and somewhat uncompromising. With infinite tact and judgment, she had retired from the Court on the arrival of the gay, pleasure-loving daughter of the Stuarts, else would her careful Teutonic soul have been scandalized at the extent of the new Electress's household, and at its spendthrift ways. On the Electress's dowry lands at Kaiserslautern, at the foot of the Hartz Mountains, and under this careful tutelage, Elizabeth's early impressions were received ; and when at ten years old she joined the Court of her mother at the Hague, she appeared a grave, demure child, who quickly earned the ridicule of her uncle Maurice.

She was undoubtedly the intellectual superior of the rest of the family ; acquired languages with ease, and showed a real talent for mathematics. Her youngest sister, the witty Electress Sophia of Hanover, mother of George I, describes her with a clear touch, in which one suspects, however, a trifle of maliciousness. " My sister," she says, " who was called Mme. Elizabeth, had black hair, a dazzling complexion, brown sparkling eyes, a well-shaped forehead, beautiful cherry lips, and a sharp acquiline nose, which was rather apt to turn red. She loved study, but all her philosophy could not save her from vexation when her nose was red. At such times she hid herself from the world. I remember that my sister, Princess Louise, who was not so sensitive, asked her on one such unlucky occasion to come upstairs to the Queen, as it was the usual hour for visiting her. Princess Elizabeth said, ' Would you have me go with this nose ? ' The other replied, ' Will you wait till you get another ? ' Louise was lively and unaffected, Elizabeth very learned ; she knew every language and every science under the sun, and corresponded regularly with Descartes.

ELIZABETH, PRINCESS PALATINE.

This great learning, however, by making her rather absent-minded, often became the subject of our mirth."

When Elizabeth was just twenty, she rejected the suit of the King of Poland rather than abjure the religion of which her father had so long been the representative. The restoration of Frederick to his dignities— never to be accomplished—was destined to symbolize the triumph of the Protestant cause in Europe. This decision was owing to Elizabeth having at that time commenced her true intellectual life. She had begun to think out truth for herself. Two years earlier, had been published the *Discours de la Méthode* of Descartes, and the young student eagerly devoured it, as well as the *Essaies*, and the *Méditations*, which shortly followed.

Another contemporaneous description of Elizabeth, will give a glimpse of the reverse side of her character, to that drawn by her sister. Sorbière, a famous French physician, who lived for many years in Holland, says :— " Wonders are told of this rare personage. It is said that to the know- ledge of strange tongues, she has added that of abstruse sciences, that she is not to be satisfied with the mere pedantic terms of scholastic lore, but will dive down to the clearest possible comprehension of things ; that she has a sharp wit, and a most solid judgment ; that she enjoys listening to Descartes, and studies his works far into the night ; that she likes surgical experiments, and causes dissections to be made before her eyes ; and lastly that in her palace dwells a clergyman suspected of being a Socinian. Her age at this time seems to be somewhere about twenty ; her beauty and carriage really those of a heroine ! "

Between Descartes and the Princess there sprang up a rare friendship. To both of them it was of incalculable worth. To Descartes, Elizabeth, with her refined intellect, showing the rare combination of mathe- tical and metaphysical powers, became at once the inspirer and critic of all he wrote from that time till his death. To the Princess, his letters, which are discretion itself, and in which he never forgets the difference in their stations, gave a stimulus to study, which nothing else could have supplied.

The position of the Princess, during the greater part of her life, was one of extreme discomfort, not to say humiliation, for a woman of her intellectual gifts. Soon after reaching maturity, she left her mother's court at the Hague, never to return, and for many years she occupied a place of complete dependence in the court of her brother, Charles Louis, Elector Palatine, at Heidelberg. With the Elector's wife, she had very little in common, yet with a faithfulness characteristic of her nature, she espoused the latter's cause with warmth and discretion, during the long course of neglect and ill-treatment which she suffered at the hands of her husband. At length, in April, 1667, Charles Louis did procure for his sister the appointment of Abbess at the well-endowed Lutheran convent of Herwerden, or Herford, in Westphalia. This post conferred on her a certain political dignity, and she became nominally a member of the German Empire. She was authorized to send a deputy to the Diet, and required to furnish one horseman and six foot soldiers to the Imperial forces. She presided in a court of justice, and exercised authority over some 7,000 persons, in the Imperial town of Herford, and the adjacent villages. Her territory became the asylum for many persecuted religionists, and it was the establishment there of the followers of Jean de Labadie, that led to an acquaintance between the Princess and the English Friends, which resulted in warm friend-ship, especially with William Penn, who says in one of his letters to her, "Thou hast taught me to forget that thou art a Princess."

Penn probably visited Herford on his first journey to Holland in 1671. Barclay and Benjamin Furly also visited the Princess in 1676, so that on Penn's second visit in 1677, she and her companion, the Countess Hornes, were amply prepared to receive him as the friend of Barclay, her kinsman. For through his mother, Catherine, daughter of Sir Robert Gordon, the first Knight Baronet of Scotland, Gentleman of the Bedchamber, and second cousin to James I., Barclay was clearly connected with the Princess by ties of blood as well as friendship. Upon the imprisonment of his father, Colonel David Barclay, and many more Friends in Scotland, Robert Barclay wrote to the Princess to request her brother, Prince Rupert, to use his influence for their release. Her answer, dated July 11st, 1676, says, "I should admire God's providence, if my brother could be a means of releasing your father and forty more in Scotland : having promised to do his best, I know he will perform it. He has ever been true to his word." In the same letter, she begs that any of the Friends will visit her. A few months later, Robert Barclay himself lay in the Tolbooth of Aberdeen, for attending meeting with some other Friends, and Elizabeth wrote again to Prince Rupert, begging him to prevent their destruction. ("Diary of Alexander Jaffray," p. 355.) Barclay also requested the Princess to use her influence with the Duchess of Lauderdale, whose husband was a member of the Scotch Council, and high in favour with Charles II., for the relief of the Friends in Scotland from persecution.

There was always a welcome for the Friends at Herford, and among those who visited the Princess beside the above were Gertrude Dericks, Elizabeth Hendricks, Isabel Yeomans, daughter of Judge Fell, and the wife of George Keith.

An interesting account of Penn's visit to her is to be found in his Journal of his "Travels in Holland and Germany," 4th ed., pp. 19-30. A vivid picture of her life of daily, unostentatious charity is drawn by him in "No Cross, No Crown," among his short biographical accounts called "Serious Dying as well as Living Testimonies." He says :—

"The late Princess Elizabeth of the Rhine of right claimeth a memorial in this discourse, her virtue giving greater lustre to her name than her quality, which yet was of the greatest in the German empire. She chose a single life as freest from care and best suited to the study and meditation she always inclined to ; and the chiefest diversion she took, next the air, was in some such plain and housewifely entertainment, as knitting, &c. She had a small territory, which she governed so well that she showed herself fit for a greater. She would constantly, every last day of the week, sit in judgment and hear and determine causes herself, where her patience, justice, and mercy were admirable, frequently remitting her forfeitures, where the party was poor, or otherwise meritorious. And which was excellent though unusual, she would temper her religion, and strangely draw concerned parties to submission and agreement, exercising not so much the rigour of her power as the power of her persuasion. Her meekness and humility appeared to me extraordinary. She never considered the quality but the merit of the people she entertained. Did she hear of a retired man hid from the world, and seeking after the knowledge of a better, she was sure to set him down in the catalogue of her charity if he wanted it. I have casually seen, I believe, fifty tokens sealed and superscribed to the several poor subjects of her bounty, whose distance would not suffer them to know one another, though they knew her, whom yet some of them had never seen. Thus, though she kept no sumptuous table in her own court, she spread the tables of the poor in their solitary cells, breaking bread to virtuous pilgrims according to their want and her ability. Abstemious in herself and in apparel, void of all vain ornaments.

" She lived her single life till about sixty years of age, and then departed at her own house in Herwerden 11th of 2nd Mo., 1680, as much lamented as she had lived beloved of her people. To whose real worth, I do, with a religious gratitude for her kind reception, dedicate this memorial."

23. Epistle to Friends, in Dutch, signed Jacob Aerents, Jan Roelofs, Bade van Tongere, Peter Hendricks, and Jan Claus, dated 11th of 1st Mo., 1680, Holland style.

Reports on the state of affairs, mentions disbursements for Friends at Embden and Dantzic, and states sums in hand.

24. Copy, in his own hand, of a letter from Crisp to Penn, dated London, 4th of 3rd Month (May), 1684. It was carried out by the *Endeavour*, and received by Penn at Philadelphia in July, 1684. (Clarkson's "Life of Penn," Vol. I., p. 419.)

He has a great sense of the intricate cares, and multiplicity of affairs, of different kinds, which daily attend one in such a responsible position. Reminds him that natural parts alone cannot advance the interest and profit of the government, and plantation, and at the same time give the interests of Truth due preference in all things. The eyes of men are upon him ; may he be furnished with wisdom. The writer has not been in London since last Yearly Meeting, when he was taken with a fit of the stone, lasting three weeks. In the winter he lost his dear wife. His body grows crazy and weakly, but he is in good courage and confidence, concerning the main business he is continued for, viz., the service of God and His people. The country about Colchester is quiet, but several meetings are laid by for fear ; theirs are exceedingly large ; many have been lately convinced. Their dear friend Gertrude*[*] is still at his house, a careful nurse for him. She is at Colchester, but will come to the Yearly Meeting. "Dear William, I might write long till all were written that lies in my heart, but, *in summa*, I love thee well, and salute thee dearly in y^t which is unchangeable."

25. The judgment on one Guin (Gwyn), Mayor of Smith-ick, not far from Plymouth, a new corporation, "soe made since the king came in."

26. A copy of No. 105.

105. John Lodge to Crisp, dated Amsterdam, "11th of the mo. called March, 1669, N. Style." ("Collectitiæ," p. 151.)

He had prepared himself against S. C. as against a day of battle. Had thought the foundation of his house stood sure, but was made to know he was but a tottering wall. Has news from England, that William Welsh and others now judged what before they contended for, viz., the hat testimony. Relates how, through an extraordinary mental conflict, he came to see the powerful work begun in England, his strong oaks bowed as a young twig, his spears turned into sickles. Wishes a copy sent to William Welsh, John Osgood, Gawen Lawry, and John Pennyman, or it may be read in public or private.

---

[*] This is Gertrude Dericks, of Amsterdam, whom, two years later, Crisp married.

Gawen Lawry, or Lawrie, was a London merchant, who also probably owned property in Hertfordshire, since his goods were there seized. (Besse, i., 252). Some time after 1680, he was appointed by Robert Barclay, Deputy Governor to the province of East Jersey, with a salary of £400, Barclay himself being Governor. He was also joint trustee with Penn, and Nicholas Lucas, for the assignment of West Jersey for the benefit of the creditors of Bylinge, the proprietor. (Jaffray's Diary, p. 363.)

27 and 28. See Jan Claus, 19.

29 and 30. Two Epistles in Dutch, from Crisp, to Friends in Holland, dated Amsterdam, 28th of 4th Month (June), 1667, Old Style; and London, 6th of 12th Mo., 1667 (Feb., 1668).

31. Letter from Dorothy Storr, to Crisp, dated Owstwicke, East Riding, Yorks, 8th of 1st Month (March).

In the Lord is safe hiding place, in this their stormy day. May they endure with patience the sharpness and greatness of their deep sufferings, which her spirit hath had a feeling of. They received Stevens letter, which was cause of joy, also heaviness, since he is in prison. It is greatly desired that he write as soon as he has freedom. Her husband salutes him, and she is straitened for time. [Adds in a postcript] "The storm doth not yet reach us, but we look for it. Heare is a great calme at present in these parts. J. W. is at home, and W. D. a prisoner at Warwick, but hath some libertie at present. G. F. prisoner, Lancaster."

Dorothy Storr was the wife of Marmaduke Storr, of Beeford, Holderness, Yorks, grazier. His brother, Joseph Storr, being in prison at Northampton in 1654, Marmaduke went to visit him, on his way into Staffordshire to renew the lease of his farm, the rental of which was about £140 per annum. On arriving at Northampton, he was thrown into prison, for refusing the oath of allegiance, which of course the magistrates had no right to tender him. He was thus prevented from visiting his landlord, so that his family were obliged to remove themselves, their stocks, and cattle from his farm at a day's notice, "to his grievous loss and disadvantage." It appeared at his trial, that he had been engaged in serving the Commonwealth in its direst straits, " for which," said he, "they are indebted to me about two hundred pounds, as my commission, debenture, and claims on record will show." Nevertheless, he was arrested on the pretext of being a person disaffected to the government, and was detained in prison ten months.

The writer of No. 71, Dorothy Hutchinson, was the daughter of

Marmaduke and Dorothy Storr, married 29th of May, 1668, to Thomas Hutchinson, of Beverley.

W. D. William Dewsbury was in prison nine years at Warwick, and finally died there, but in his own house, June, 1688. Fox was a prisoner in Lancaster from 1663 to 1665.

32. Theodor Eccleston to Crisp, dated London, 29th of 7th Mo. (Sept.), 1691 ; enclosing " the Heads of the Deed " of Trust, of a meeting-house and burial ground, at Swansea, dated 17th of March, 1674.

He is often sending him papers, because he loves to have something wherewith to visit him. The grandson of the donor [of meeting-house, etc.] now sues for it, pleading part of the Statute of Mortmain. Friends' counsel insists on the equitable part ; the judge is of opinion that the trust is good, so long as any of the trustees are living. He asks Steven for his sense of the law, that he may advise them.

Sewel, in his Preface, p. xii, thanks his " well-beloved and much esteemed friend, THEODOR ECCLESTON, of London, who has furnished me with abundance of materials not only useful, but absolutely necessary for the compiling of this work."   Whitehead calls him his " deare friend," and says: " He lent me his gelding, being a good easy horse, and I being but weakly, and time being precious," for the journey to Highclere, Hants, the seat of Sir Robert Sawyer, the Attorney-General, to obtain from him signature to the warrant delivered to Barclay and himself, 15th March, 1685-6, for the release of the Friends in prison at that time. (" Christian Progress," Lond. 1725, 8vo., p. 590.)

In December, 1694, Theodor Eccleston drew up, and signed on behalf of the Society, " A brief representation of the Quakers' case of not swearing ; and why they might have been, and yet may be, relieved therein by Parliament."   This was presented to Parliament, but they came to no resolution in favour of the quakers, yet individual members thereof " discovered a more friendly regard toward them." (Gough's " History," iii. 370-8.) Eccleston died at Mortlake in 1726. His son, John Eccleston, became noted in trade in the city of London, and was a Director of the East India Company.

33. Letter from Judith Zinspenning, in Dutch, to Crisp, dated Amsterdam, the 2nd of 5th Mo. (July), 1664. See No. 141.

She salutes him in love.   Ed. Roelofs is ill with some fever, probably measles, also his children.   Her son William is still very weak.   She greets Edward de Kleermaker, his wife and children, Solomon [? Freemantel] and his wife, Crisp's father and mother, and all others, when he is free. Especial love to Felis Waraedistel; if her letter seems refreshing to him, let it be also to his fellow-prisoners.

JUDITH ZINSPENNING was the mother of Sewel the historian, a woman of great gifts, and whose early acquirements were so unusual that her father used to say, "It is a pity this girl was not a boy, that she might in time become an eminent instrument in the Church." Her son gives some interesting particulars of her early life in his "History of the Rise," etc. (vol. II. pp. 68, 121-5), and tells us that she was much sought after by the professors, and Fifth Monarchy men, on account of her natural abilities. In 1663, she visited England with William Caton, his wife, and another Friend, and spoke at a meeting at Kingston, William Caton being her interpreter. She afterwards stayed in London, where on one occasion, she preached with such power, that although the only interpreter present was not equal to the occasion, many "testified to the life and power that accompanied her speech." She wrote several small books, including a book of Proverbs, translated into English by William Caton, and published in London 1663, with a note appended, that it is "to be sent among the chosen generation in England, but especially in Essex, London, and about Kingstone," which places she had most visited. She also penned many Epistles to Friends, one of which Sewel gives. (Vol. ii. pp. 125-8.)

34. Crisp to John Wilkinson, in Spalding Prison, from Lincoln. (The corner with the date is torn off.)

Although he has never seen his face, he is drawn to write to him. Having been ordered to pass through Friends in Yorkshire, he has, in divers places, heard of him. Proceeds to advise to humility, and amendment of life.

35. A paper in Dutch; possibly a rough copy of an epistle; no date or signature.

36. "A note of what has lately happened among the Menuists."

A list of occurrences in East Friesland, Hamburg, Harlingen, Amsterdam, Haarlem, and Dantzic, whereby the strife among these sectarians is related.

The MENNONITES (called generally in this Collection, Menuists) were a portion of the Anabaptist section of the church, opposed to the more violent and fanatical party. They took their name from Menno Simons, born in 1492, at Witmarsum, Holland, and originally ordained a Romish priest. In 1536 he left the Romish church, and became one of the Baptists, whose constancy under persecution he had seen. Many vigorous churches were founded by him and his followers, in Friesland, Holstein, Cologne, and Zurich. He died in 1559. The Mennonites reject infant baptism, oaths, the bearing of arms, and all unnecessary ornaments in dress. They consider that human learning does not qualify for the ministry, and that no hire should be given to ministers, although the congregations assist their pastors with the means of living, if poor. Their meeting-houses were very plain, with galleries for the ministers. They practise silent prayer in meetings, and are in many respects, as will thus be seen, identical in practice and belief with the teachings of Fox. The resemblance may be further studied in Barclay's " Inner Life of the Commonwealth," London, 1876. See also letter No. 19, from Hilary Prache, and notes following on Schwenksfeld and his followers, and the Collegianten, two other branches of the Mennonites.

37.   Paper in Dutch, relating to R. Barclay, dated Amsterdam, 13th of 8th Mo. (Oct.), 1677.

38.   Copy of the deed to be signed by all masters of ships at the Brill, the port of Rotterdam.

" Wee underwritten master and masters mate, designed with the help of God to sayle to England, doe hereby attest and declare, that there is noe more nor other goods, wares, nor merchantdise, to our knowledge, loaden in the ship now under our command, then onely those that are exprest in these our °Cocquets, which we do here exhibit, and deliver over to the Commissioners of ye utmost yuard of ye Netherlands, at Recherche, for them thereby to make search and visitation. And that noe fraud is acted, that we know of, nor that none of the goods laden in our ship is silenced, or any indeavour used directly or indirectly to wrong or hinder ye rights and priviledges of this country. And further we doe holyly and uprightly promise, that after the Commissioners at Recherche have made their visitation, we will take into our ship noe other nor any more goods, nor suffer any to be laden, unlesse they be first given over, and lawfully entered at the Custom House, and that it doth so appear to us by the Passports, or Cocquets, that such goods shall be delivered to us ; that by our knowledge the rights and customs of this country may not directly or indirectly be hindered or shortened. In witness whereunto we have signed this with our owne hands this—— day of——.

This is a true copy, of ye printed paper which ye English masters sets their hands to, at ye Brill, when they come away. Translated for Information of such, as for want of understanding the Dutch tongue, sets their hands to they know not what, and often promise, attest, and declare thereby, more than is true, and soe brings a burden upon themselves."

---

* Cocquets :—An official custom-house warrant description of certain goods which the searcher may pass to be shipped.

39. Printed advice from the Meeting for Sufferings, dated 20th of 10th Mo. (Dec.), 1769, signed William Weston.

40. A short and simple answer to ten questions, given forth by N. N. N. 'Written in great haste by me, John Vanderwey.'

68. A Dutch translation of the same, signed John Vander Wedye.

41. See No. 12.

42. Copy of a Prophecy sent to Benjamin Furly, of Rotterdam, in the year 166—, from Montpelier, by the late Honourable Algernon Sydney, Esq., and by him, the said B. Furly, accidentally found among old papers this 18th of 8th Mo. (Oct.), 1688.—See Nos. 10 and 104, B. Furly.

42* and 43. Two long and closely written letters, signed T. H., dated Beverley, 6th, and 17th of 7th Mo. (Sept.), 1679, and dealing with some dispute about the sale of a piece of land, mortgaged by the writer to G. Lawry (see No. 26), and G. Hutchinson.

The case is to be tried in Chancery, and he is anxious to present certain papers. He will send his wife by coach to London, and if S. C. will render her assistance as a friend, he will take it kindly. Has given her full power and instructions to act. Thinks that he has been hardly judged by Friends. Swims in the waters of affliction which rise higher and higher over his head. Hopes a friend may be raised to stand by his wife.

These letters, the most puzzling in the whole Collection, I take to be from Thomas Hutchinson, husband of Dorothy Storr, to whom she addresses the letter No. 71. If so, they were written on the eve of his starting for Maryland, and contain no hint of his intended desertion. But they are extremely ill written and spelt, and contain such repetition of his hard treatment by Friends, that it is impossible to follow the story. He deprecates judgment of him, and a letter from Friends of Hull, directed to Steven Crisp, at William Crouch's; asks Crisp to reserve judgment, and, with G. Whitehead and Alexander (? Parker) to assist him, and rebuke G. Lawry.

44. No paper.

45. Articles of agreement between Crisp and John Cannon, the elder, of Clothall, in the county of Hertfordshire, respect-

ing the falling and sale of timber in Bryan's wood, dated 3rd of October, 1674.

45*a*. Copy of a paper, signifying that whereas Mathias Harmun, tailor, of Haarlem, has for seven or eight years been rebellious against all efforts for his reformation from disorderly and unruly practices, they, the General Meeting of Amsterdam, held the 23rd of 8th Mo. (Oct.), 1670, do declare they have no longer any fellowship with him.

45*b*. A similar testimony against Bowdin Bowdenune, of Leyden.

46. Similar denial of Mar : M.; of Mart : Cuyper ; Walter Arents, of Rotterdam, and Mary, his wife; and Isaac Furnerius, of Rotterdam, apostates, with whom they have laboured in vain.

FURNERIUS was a doctor, who though at first a Friend, became afterwards a Papist. See Caton's letter, No. 141, also Sewel's History, 4th ed., 1799, p. 232.

47. Letter to the burgomaster of Landtsmeer, in the Netherlands, in Dutch, signed Peter Hendricks (see No. 18), and Jacob Bects.

47*a*. Extract from Episcopius on the xvii. John, pp. 30, 31.

SIMON EPISCOPIUS (1583-1643), Professor of Divinity at Leyden University, was a pupil of Arminius.

47*b*. The sad end of Canon James Latemus, Doctor and Professor of Divinity at Leyden, 29th of May, 1546.

47*c* and 48. Burning at the stake of John de Bakker, priest, of Woerden, on the 15th of September, 1525, aged twenty-seven, the first martyr in Holland.

49. Forty queries given forth in Germany, in the 5th Mo. (July), 1657, by an Englishman, George Rofe.

102. George Rofe to Crisp, dated Barbadoes, 16th of 9th Mo. (Nov.), 1661.

He has been made an instrument of good in those countries. Has visited Maryland, Virginia, New England, and the islands thereabout, also the island of Bermuda, in all of which places there are many Friends. Is now settled in the fruitful island of Barbadoes, which may be called the nursery of the truth. A meeting is held there every day, and sometimes two or three. Is glad to hear of the increase and prosperity of Friends in Colchester, and wishes to greet them as if named one by one. Will be glad to hear how it is with all those counties, and may be addressed to Thomas Hart, Bridgetown, Barbadoes, where he may stay some time.

GEORGE ROFE was born at Halsted in Essex, and was a glazier there. As early as 1655, he was preaching at Hythe, in Kent, from which place he narrowly escaped with his life, being thrown by the violence of the crowd down some steep stone stairs, and otherwise ill-treated in the presence of the Mayor, for having, after the priest had done, exhorted the people. The next year he was in Bury St. Edmund's gaol, whence he dated " Sion's Rock exalted over all the Earth to reign," published 1656. In 1658 he was confined for five months in the prison at Saffron Walden, for speaking to a priest in the church. He also wrote " The Revelation of God," pub. 1658, dated from Ipswich gaol December of the year preceding ; " Cherubims," dated Barbadoes, 1661 ; and "A Demonstration through the Eternall Spirit," 1663. He was drowned during a storm on Maryland River, in a small boat, at the beginning of the year 1664. (See letters from Caton, Nos. 135 and 141.)

50. Objections to the proposed laws of New Jersey Settlement, whereby an inhabitant, and freeholder, was excluded from the Assembly, if he held land in any other part of America.

51. Extract from an old Chronicle of Holland, showing how, in 814, Charles Ludovick, Emperor and Earl of Holland, married his niece.

52. No paper.

53. Letter from John Furly, to the men's meeting in Colchester, dated Colch., 10th Mo. (Dec.), 1710.

He is unable to be with them, but wishes John Hawkins to have ¾ ton of coal out of Susan Shortland's gift ; also Thomas Brown has paid for ¾ ton to B. Freeman's daughter by mistake ; let it be rectified.

This is the son of John Furly, mayor of Colchester in 1680.

54. Twenty-nine closely written pages of Crisp's autobiography, pp. 1-53 of Crisp's *Works*, ed. Field, London, 1694.

55. Objections against the articles of the planters of Carolina.

It is impossible, according to the present Constitutions published, for those to keep a good conscience who are called quakers . . . if they submit thereunto. Seven reasons are given. "As concerning the policys established for government, they concerne ourselves not much therein, their kingdome being not of this world, seeking onely that under whomsoever they live, their lives may be godly and quiett. To voluntaryly transplant themselves from their native countrys, where they have indured such great persecutions for keeping conscience cleere, and now, by a voluntary subscription in a strange country, to cast away that liberty which, through God's goodness and ye king's clemency, they have obtained in their owne, would not be prudence to themselves, nor safe for their posterity, and therefore they propound, for their owne safeguard, and the quiett and peace of their consciences, these following expedients" :—

Here follow six propositions, desiring that no Quaker shall be examined concerning his faith, provided he doe not endeavour the damage of any other in person or property ; that their affirmation yea or nay shall pass for another's oath ; that they shall keep their own registers, and deliver duplicates before the judges at every assizes, to be there entered ; that they shall not be constrained to beare armes ; that none to whom the above exemptions refer shall be held incapable of bearing any office or dignity to which he may be properly chosen ; and that none shall be constrained to maintaine any ministers of another church than his own.

56. Letter from Simon de Pool to Crisp, in Dutch, dated Amsterdam, 11th of May, 1674, and addressed to him in Rotterdam.

Has acted as interpreter to the Polish Envoy, returning home after his travels in France, England, the Hague. He goes by Copenhagen to Warschau, in Poland. One Albertus Opauki, a learned man, perfect in the Latin tongue. Took him by desire to the Meeting, he was well pleased, and bought some buttons.

One Simon van der Pyl was minister of the English church at Flushing for thirty-two years, from 1700. He may have been a son of Crisp's correspondent. (Stevens' "History of Scotch Church in Rotterdam," Edin., 1832, p. 306.)

57. See Furly, No. 10.

58. Michael Mugge to his two sons, Michael and Jacob, in German, dated Dantzic, the 12th day of 9th Mo. (Nov.), 1683.

He understands his dear children are well and happy in Holland, and to hear of them from Friends is comforting, but that they follow those evil ones of Dantzic is not good. It is better to live in freedom than to be in the house of correction. He would be glad if they could come back to him, if it is the Lord's will. His affectionate love to them and all Friends.

Michael Mugge's wife is mentioned in Besse's "Sufferings," Vol. ii., p. 434, as being imprisoned in Dantzic, and released by the intercession of Christian Andreas, citizen of Dantzic, who relates the occurrence in a letter to Jan Claus, dated 22nd January, 1678.

59. Copy, in Dutch, of a letter from Theodorus Poludamus, preacher, of Leeuwarden, to the Lady Habuerin, dated Leeuwarden, the 10th November, 1681.

64. Translation into English of the same, by Crisp, containing a detailed account of the burning of Dowee Sitses, mason, of Bolsward [Friesland], who, while lying drunk upon his kitchen floor, was burned, as the writer conceives, in response to his own repeated oaths, and herein a judgment upon all drunkards is implied. He has been with the Procuror General to investigate the case ; found two master chirurgeons and their assistants dressing the patient. In response to the desire of her ladyship, these particulars are forwarded.

60. Copy, in Crisp's writing, of an award in a controversy concerning the will of Neisy Dericks, the sister of Crisp's second wife, Gertrude Losevelt.

Her will is that 3,000 gulden shall be set apart for the service of friends in the ministry, and for the furtherance of the truth professed by the people called Quakers. In pursuance of this, her sister Gertrude Dericks [who was sole heire] hath by her transport, made in 1665, divided and separated the said 3,000 gulden from the rest of the estate, and hath committed the rule of the same to Wm. C[aton] ; J. Ff[urly] ; C[ornelius] R[oelofs] and P[eter] H[endricks], to be by them disposed of according to the will of the late Neisy Dericks ; howbeit the said capitall is now lying so scattered, that it is not in a condition to answer the ends aforesaid. Also, some controversy having arisen between Gertrude D., and C. R., and P. H., concerning the security, for the ending of the same, G. D. with her husband, Adrian Van Loosevelt, on the one part, and C. R. and P. H., on the other part, have given up the matters relating thereunto to J. C[laus] and S. C[risp], by a writing under all their hands in the presence of witnesses, promising to stand to whatever they shall settle, and for the ending of all controversy for ever, they, chosen by the parties in difference, do decide as follows : that Isaac Jacobs, Jacob Arents, and Gertrude Dericks of Amsterdam, doe receive the severall sums of money out of divers hands hereafter mentioned, viz :—

468 gulden from Ad. V. Loosevelt.

500 gulden from Lambert Person, with interest.

350 gulden of R. Teetes.

1,052 gulden of Cornelius Roelofs, and 350 gulden of the widow of Barent Roelofs, but if the said widow cannot conveniently pay at present, then the appoyntment is that she give to the said three such security as they shall approve and accept.

These sums having been received, the three trustees shall re-invest the same, and at all times when any Friends in the ministry shall come to this country, they shall give them out of it what sums they require to make use of. And further, it is ordered that the trustees shall record in a book, all their receipts and disbursement, "that noe grounds may be for jealousies and objections." In case of the death of any of the trustees, notice shall be given to the Friends in the ministry to appoint another in their room. This is the determination of the arbitrators, that so peace and order may ensue instead of strife, and that there may be no more stumbling-block.

And if Gertrude Dericks be not in a capacity to supply the needs of Leisy Thomas, and Mary Jansen, then, once a year, the said three trustees may advance forty guldens a-piece to the said Leisy, and Mary, towards their maintenance, as long as their necessity continue.

61. Letter from John Blaykling to Crisp, dated Drawell, 14th of 6th Mo. (Aug.).

He received Crisp's three days ago, and is glad they have been kept in faithfulness. He travails with his friends in their trials and afflictions. As Crisp has wisdom and dominion amongst them, let him be as a lamb, serving in brokenness of heart, to the strengthening of the feeble. His love and yearning is to all in the immortal birth, that hold fast their testimony. When Crisp is writing to John Furly,° he wishes to be remembered, for he is dear to him. His love is also to Thomas Bayles, and others whose names he does not know.

JOHN BLAYKLING was a native of Drawell, in the parish of Sedbergh, Yorks, born in 1625, a minister for fifty years. He was many times imprisoned in York, and Tynemouth Castles, and elsewhere. At his house was held the meeting which began on the 3rd of April, 1676, and lasted four days, for the recovery of Storey and Wilkinson, two turbulent persons who had set aside the good order and discipline of the Society, saying they were forms. Blaykling wrote " Antichristian Treachery Discovered," and died at the age of eighty, 4th May, 1705.

62. See Hendricks, 18.

63. A long document in Dutch, addressed to Pieter Arents, and signed Cornelius Roelofs.

64. See 59.

65. See Hendricks, 18.

66. Relation of a prophetic vision, seen by Eervert Lückes, of Stoneven, while asleep on board a vessel at Amsterdam, the 2nd of 10th Mo. (Dec.), 1653.

The decline of Holland is foretold, the war with Cromwell, the Covenant with the Spanish Netherlands, and the death of Gustavus Adolphus, after which " shall Cromwell's generation hold up of reigning, and England shall seek a king, not out of a strange

---

* As Furly lived at Colchester, this remark and the tenour of the letter seems to indicate that it was, like many others of the Collection, addressed to Crisp while in prison.

nation, but he that now is fled. Then shall great joy prevail in Holland, for they shall make a covenant, but it shall not long endure, for war shall follow and losses at sea, with great strivings by land and sea. After which the king of France shall prosper and attain much power over the Friesland countries, but when the anguish is at the height, there shall come a swift deliverance, at a time when it is least seen. Thus far the vision of the dream."

67. **Remarkable cure of Jeske Claes, wife to Rinck Abbis, boatman upon the Princes Island, Amsterdam, by a vision on the night of the 13th of October, 1676. Translated from the printed copy, published at New Bridge St., Amsterdam, in 1677.**

For fourteen years she had been a cripple, in one leg no feeling, no strength in the other, forced to creep on the floor, be drawn in a little waggon, or carried in arms like a child. On the night between the 13th and 14th of October, 1676, she heard the clock strike, and the rattle watch cry out one o'clock. She lay on her side and dozed, but felt something grasp her right wrist three times, and a voice said, "Thy goings shall be restored to thee again." She sate up on end, and cried, "Shall I, sinful creature, be so happy as to have my going restored?" and the answer came, "It shall be so, but keep it private at present." Then she cried still more loudly (so that the neighbours overhead heard her), "Lord, had I but light to see what happens to me!" and, taking hold of her husband, sought to wake him, but in vain.

Then the voice said, "Light shall be given thee," and immediately a brightness shone through the chamber, and she saw as plain as one can see another, a little lad of about the size of ten years, with yellow, curled hair, short like the hair of the blacks, and a white garment down to his feet, with another white garment, which hung in flat pleats above the first. He took two steps towards her, and then, neither of them having breathed a word, vanished. Then she cried, "Lord, am I but to enjoy thy light for so short a time?" And next, she felt like a stream of luke-warm water, in her right hip and toe, and exclaimed, "I have life where I had none before."

As soon as her husband was gone, she rose up and thought to stand, but alas! she could not, and in her despair, she wept, until the neighbours wondered. Now, two days after, she sat in her kitchen, trying to boil some fish and sour soup for her husband's mother, who lay sick, when again the voice said, "Thy going is given thee, go and meet thy husband." Which doing, he was amazed, and affrighted, and said, "Thou art not she," thinking it were a spirit, and retreated before her, until she clasped her hands about his neck. In the meantime, there entered her daughter, bearing a candle, and stood speechless, not knowing what this should mean. Upon which, her husband cried, "Is this thy mother?" "Yea, father," she faltered. He, with much doubting, stretched out his hand, saying, "If thou beest my wife, I give thee my hand in God's name."

"Whosoever desires further satisfaction herein, may have the account from her own mouth, as long as it please God she lives."

This extraordinary story recalls the visions of Mrs. Jane Lead (1623-1704), who has been called the last of the English visionaries, and who was the author of many mystical treatises, and the founder of the Society of Philadelphians. Her remarkable life and death, at the age of eighty-one, having been blind for many years, are related in the letters of her son-in-law, the learned Dr. Francis Lee, and may be studied with great advantage, in a sympathetic article by Canon R. C. Jenkins (British Quarterly, July, 1873, pp. 181-7), by any one interested in the history of Mysticism.

68. A Dutch translation of No. 40.

69. Copy of an Epistle, from William Dewsbury, given forth the 22nd of 3rd Month (May), 1657, in Kent ; also of a short note of counsel from him, dated Warwick, 5th of 3rd Mo. (May), 1671.

WILLIAM DEWSBURY, one of the earliest followers of Fox, was born at Allerthorpe, Yorks, in 1621. He was apprenticed to a cloth weaver, and afterwards joined the parliamentary army. He was imprisoned altogether nineteen years, at York, Derby, Northampton, Newgate, and Warwick, in which place, he was, for the third time, imprisoned from 1678, until the general proclamation of James II., 1685. He died 17th June, 1688.

70. A long, and exquisitely written letter, in Dutch, from Elizabeth Hendricks to Crisp, no date.

ELIZABETH HENDRICKS travelled about preaching. She wrote an " Epistle to Friends in England," published at Amsterdam, 1672, and others in Dutch. In 1677 she and Gertrude Dericks, afterwards Crisp, visited the Princess Elizabeth, and the Labadists at Herford. Some account of this remarkable sect, and its founder, Jean de Labadie, is to be found in an account of the Princess by the editor, *British Friend*, July, 1890.

71. Copy of a letter from Dorothy Hutchinson, formerly Storr (see No. 31), to her husband, in Maryland, dated Owst-wicke, East Rid., Yorks., 26th of 3rd Mo. (May), 1680.

This letter, which shows us a wife of strict integrity and brave spirit, reasoning with a vain, spendthrift, and insolvent husband, who in pursuance of his " airy shadows " has set sail for the West, leaving his wife and three children in the depths of poverty, increased by her rigid care to repay their creditors, is printed at length in *Collectitiæ*, W. Alexander & Sons, York, 1824, p. 245.

72. Letter from Joseph Campagne, a French Protestant refugee, to Crisp, no date.

He has received, from one of the brethren, a discourse written by Crisp for the comfort and instruction of the French refugees, and proceeds to criticise the same. Quotes Pagans and Christians in support of the theory of the light of conscience. Solomon, though of such an amorous temper that he became a slave to his wives, is a notable example of the result of a good education and breeding. Self-interest is the power that has seduced half the French Protestants into popery, it keeps bishops, priests, and monks in the false worship of the Romish Church, and perhaps 'tis that which hinders the Reformed Doctors from joining this Society whose ministry is performed *gratis*. Salmeron, and Maldonat,[*] the Jesuits, affirm that either the gospel, or pomp, luxury, and wealth must be thrown off, because the gospel bids the distribution of superfluous estates to the poor. Therefore let all Christian Societies have all things common among them, like the first believers. Fourthly, with the remarks concerning the imprudence of such as give themselves to be governed by pastors and teachers he has much accord, and indeed is so drawn towards the Society of which Crisp is a member, that he would be directed to some of the brethren in London who may take care of him. Address him at Mr. Boucher's in Grafton Street.

The discourse above alluded to is :—" Charitable advice : by way of letter to the French Protestants, into what parts of the world soever dispersed by reason of their present sufferings and persecutions from the hands of the Roman Catholics," London, 1688. First written in French, one edition printed "chez Jacob Claus, Marchand Libraire, dans le Prince-straat, Amst., 1688."

73. An address to the Mayor, Aldermen, and Common Council of Harwich, dated from Harwich Common Gaol, the 27th of 12th Mo., 1661 (Feb., 1662), signed by Edward Boyce, Will. Mar[tin], Mary Vanderwall, and Steven Crisp, shewing the injustice, and inexpediency, of the harsh treatment they have received.

The charter of the town is endangered by any unjust or illegal proceedings taken by the magistrates under cover of it. In saying that their meetings are illegal, the Council doth exceed its province, seeing it yet remaineth a question in Parliament whether they shall be tolerated or nay, and for them to suppress a meeting before Parliament hath determined it, will be looked upon as a bold intrusion, and will tend to their dishonour. Sir John Shaw hath said in Colchester (where meetings are sometimes very large), that they may be held until prohibited by Parliament, which there is just cause to believe will never be, they having the word of a king for it.

74. Extract from Foxe's Acts and Monuments. Vol. ii. p. 417.

---

[*] Spanish Jesuits, born 1515 and 1534, authors of many works.

75. See 19. Jan Claus.

76. A Briefe Journall of my Travells into Germany, from Amsterdam, begun the 6th of the 4th Mo., called June, 1669, signed S. Crisp (the mark for a city thus, △).

With Claus, his interpreter, and others, Crisp travelled to Utrecht, Arnheim, Altenburgh, and by Shinkenshause (a great fort belonging to the States), and Cleves, to the house of Mary Ann Boome. Then through Regensburg, and Mors, to Ordingen, where Ludovic, the Wacht-meister, received them kindly. After visiting other places, they reached Dusseldorf, where, it being the day called Whitsun Monday, the Papists were carrying their breaden god in high procession, and they had like to have been murdered for not doffing their hats ; yet their God delivered them, and they escaped to the great city of Collon [Cologne], where they were again in danger, but embarked that night for Metz. Next day they proceeded to Bonn, Lenz, and by Boppart, to St. Geweere [St. Goar]. The following day to Bacharach, and Bingen, where the boat was exchanged for a waggon, and they drove through Werstadt, a city depopulated and spoiled in the German wars, to friends who dwell at Griesheim, two hours from Worms, to their mutuall joy. From thence they travelled to Heydelberg, to speak with the Prince Palatine about the persecution raised against Friends, by which cattle and other goods, largely exceeding in value the fine of four rix-dollars per head, were taken from them.

77. Letter from Martin John to John G. M., dated Laub-ground, 18th of 2nd Mo. (April), 1676. Endorsed " Martin John, from Selicia, about R. L.'s visit."

Is glad Roger Longworth is safe home after his visit. His labours to enforce on them silent meetings are unavailing. Although he held several, people were only attracted by curiosity to see and hear one from a far country. This Roger can not believe. Has entertained him in another's house, and kept from him all he could not bear, because he himself can both bear and forbear ; but neither he nor others will be bound either to silent or vocal meetings, and they will stand in their liberty. Sees there is not perfect agreement, since he has heard from his correspondent that they love the works of Jacob Behme, whereas Roger says though a candle was lighted in him at the beginning, yet he hunted before the Lord ; and those who have Behme's books are puffed up in their knowledge, and styled by him Behmists. Mark Shwaner remains in Sittau. He has told him their people do not receive Roger's customs and manners of worship, and no such meetings are to be set up, but hopes the journey will do both of them good, perceiving a godly people to be found in other countries, beside their own. Whilst writing, he hears Mark Shwaner is in prison, and kept so close none can come or speak to him. Every one of them, according to his measure, seeks to find God in himself. True worship is done in spirit, bound neither to place nor time. Wishes to be remembered to Roger and other friends.

78. A paper in Dutch ; very ill written, no date or signature.

79. " A dialogue between Buchanan, and Maitland, who was King James's tutor, in his minority."

80. Extract from Velthuysen, on Superstition, p. 407.

LAMBERT VaD VELTHUYSEN, a Dutch author, was born at Utrecht, 1622. His *De Idolatria et Superstitione*, &c., was published Rotterdam, 1680. He died 1685.

81. A statement by Crisp, of the will of one Nicholas Lemon, made in 1665, in favour of his wife and daughter, and in default of her issue, to his son John.

" Nicholas Lemon, in 1665, made his will, gave lands to his wife for life, and after her decease to Sara, his daughter, and ye heirs of her body, and for default of issue, to his son John, and ye heirs of his body, and for want of such issue of John, to his son Thomas, and his heirs. The wife is dead, and Sara, the daughter, is dead, and John, being possest in 1673, levyed a fine to the use of him, his heirs, and assigns for ever, and after dyes. and gives them to Margaret, his wife, for life, and after to others.

Q. Whether John, soe possest, had power to levy a fine, and by vertue thereof to dispose the estate. Memoranda.—That after ye levying the fine, John sold part of ye premisses thus given, and Thomas joyned with him in ye sale, and received twenty pounds, which was charged upon ye land payable to him by his father, and thereupon released John, his heirs, and executors, his land, and tenements.

Q. Whether, after such release, Thomas can come in for ye lands againe.

N.B. Thomas was about twenty-six yeeres old when ye fine was levied, and it is five yeeres, and three quarters, since John dyed.

Q. Whether his right to plead against ye fine by ye limitation of ye statute of fines be not expired.

Councillor Mott, please to looke over these writtings and give thy opinion in writting, whether this bearer, Solomon Owis, husband of Margrett, that was ye widow of John Lemon, have any cause to feare ye claime of Thomas Lemon, the premisses duly considered.

From thy friend, S. CRISP."

82. Copy of an Epistle from Fox, dated London, 9th of 4th Mo. (June), 1678.

84. The MSS. of Crisp's "Short History of a long travel from Babylon to Bethel," written in November, 1691, published Lond., 1711.

85. A statement of the case between Richard Barrington, and Mary Painter, his wife, whose jointure consisted of three houses, in the Liberty of Colchester, which in the siege, 1648, were burned to the ground, signed John Mosyer.

The following letter to Crisp is added :—

" Sr, immediately on receipt of yo^{rs} I went to Mr. Mosyer, who upon perusall of yor case, told me there were severall poynts of law therein, which he could not well resolve without mature deliberation, and thereupon ordered me to wait upon him this morning for his opinion, a coppy whereof I have here sent you. Hee pesents his kind respects to you and desires me to acquaint you that hee will doe all things which lyes in his power to give you full satisfaction in this matter, and to that end, after answere to ye queries, hath made severall others which he desires to be satisfied in before he can give his oppinion soe fully, as to prescribe a way for yor security. I am sorry it should be yor ill luck to meete with such a beggarly knave, who hath neither conscience nor civillity, but 'tis two common now-a-daies for such paltry ffellowes after they have spent their owne estates, to endeavour to defeate honest men of their just right, yet I doe not much doubt in this case of yo^{rs}, but that he will be disappointed. Sr, yesterday I mett with Mr. Hayes at the Parliam^t house, who hath promised to gett me yor other duplicate very speedily. I have here inclosed sent you his Maj^s speech. Mr. Seymour was chosen speaker againe, but upon his request to his maty was dismissed. I heare Sir Tho. Meers° is chose in his roome, which with my humble service to you is all at psent from Sr, yours to serve you,

NATH^L UNWIN."

London, *March 7th, 1678.*

86 and 110. Letters from John Rous, to Crisp, dated London, 1st of 11th Mo., 1677 (Jan., 1678), and Barbadoes, 13th of 3rd Mo. (May), 1679.

86. He has not forgotten about the widow Marywood's estate, that she would sell in Essex. Has learned from her it is tithe free, and she will sell it without the tithes of other estates which belong to her ; she lodges at one Hilliers in Vere Street, in New Market, near Covent Garden, where a letter may reach her. Has paid the 20s. to Willm. Brookes that was behind for interest, and taken up the obligation as desired. There is a mistake of £10 in the annuity, and a sum of £2 5s. 11d., which Thomas Yoakley received of John Bellers to pay on his account, but did not. Altogether £13 5s. 11d., which he will make up to the first half-year's interest and pay Susan, if Crisp will accept of payment through her, which may be a convenience to her. Desires to know his mind when convenient, the letter to be directed to him at Francis Bellers house in Philpot Lane. Sends love to Crisp's wife, Gertrude, and friends.

110. Crisps letter, dated 11th of 12th Mo. (Feb.), evidences the care of a faithful friend towards him. He has endeavoured to make as good an improvement of his time, in the discharge of his duties, as he could. Has done better than many expected, but has money in the hands of others, which he can not get in. It now reaches the amount of £800, which may make it difficult to call in the money he is obliged to Crisp for. He must desire patience. Will Crisp be his intercessor that it may remain till next ninth month year, or toward that time, when he may comply. In the mean-

---

* Sir Thomas Meers, Knight, sat for the city of Lincoln from 1661 to 1702.

time, he hopes to clear all engagements, so that no other encumbrance is on his house, save that Crisp has. If, however, the money cannot be longer dispensed with, he will write to John Bellers to pay. Cannot tell what losses there may be through his money passing the seas. Crisp knows the casualties and disappointments of all things, and he hopes will procure time. Is sorry to hear of so many unsavoury things, the like of the last two years has not happened in twenty before, the mouths of the enemies of the truth are opened. Men brought up to other trades can hardly hope to prosper when they go abroad, the charges of factors are so high, and goods low. Factors grow rich and get estates, while their principals are ruinated. Many ships from Ireland with beef have been in Barbadoes, but it has made less than it cost, and the loss has been great. Friends are well, truth prospers, there is frequent addition to the church, though the spirit rife in England has power there. There is the lily among thorns as well as in other places. His wife and children are well, they are about sending their oldest girl to London. His love to Crisp, and Gertrude, whose paper was read in several meetings, much to friends' satisfaction.

JOHN ROUS was the son of Lieutenant-Colonel Rous, a wealthy planter in Barbadoes. Both father and son joined the quakers. He frequently corresponded with Mrs. Fell, before making her acquaintance in 1659, on his arrival from New England, where he had been imprisoned for his opinions. He married, in March, 1661, Margaret, the eldest daughter of Judge Thomas and Margaret Fell (afterwards Fox), and settled at Kingston, Surrey, being in business in London as a West India merchant. He became the family adviser of Mrs. Fell, and assisted her during her many trials and imprisonments. John and Margaret Rous had twelve children, eight of whom died young. He was lost, with his ship, on his passage home from Barbadoes, during the month of February, 1695. (Mrs. Webb's "Fells of Swarthmoor." Lond. 1865.)

87. Letter from Crisp to John Swinton, dated Colchester, 25th of 4th Mo. (June), 1668.

Wishes, in much love, to deal with him concerning a word he heard him publicly pronounce at Stebbing, concerning those that doe slight Friends, or their testimony. Now how can he pronounce a war upon others, for doing that which he has done himself, for in his paper from Newgate the word "leaders" is three times mentioned, and it is Friends who are accused and charged. If it is not his judgment now, why is it not called in? If, as the writer hears, he maintains, that it was God's will to publish it, and he waits for the same to suppress it, can he suppose that the Lord's day and work is not certain? If he were as sensible as the writer of the harm done thereby, words would not be sufficient to obliterate what he has written. Such papers strengthen those of corrupt minds, and it is for his good that the writer has put plainly some part of what is upon him, committing him to the eternal which cannot change. Mary Vanderwall, of Harwich, is with him, and sends her dear love.

On the back of this letter, a portion of one of Fox's Epistles is copied by Crisp.

JOHN SWINTON, of Swinton, on the Borders of Scotland, was the great great grandfather, on the maternal side, of Sir Walter Scott, see letter from Sir Walter Scott in *The Friends' Monthly Magazine*, Bristol, 1830, vol. i. p. 186. He was a man in high esteem with Cromwell, and great in the management of affairs of Scotland. He held meetings with Barclay, and was imprisoned for so doing. Unfortunately he fell into great irregularity of conduct, and was for a time entirely separated from the Society, though restored upon his repentance. He died at Borthwick, 1679. (Jaffray's Diary, Lond., 1833.)°

The VANDERWALLS of Harwich were a family of Dutch origin, who intermarried with many of the English Friends. In a curious tract at Sion College, "A Reply to Tho. Upsher's pretended answer to the printed account of an occasional Conference between George·Keith and Thomas Upsher, at Colchester, the 1st of January, 1700, by George Keith," there is a history of a controversy between a Mr. Noah Raoul, of Colchester, and Daniel Vanderwall, concerning the Rule of Faith.

88. Letter from D. Harper to Crisp, dated Arksey, West Rid., Yorks, the 3rd of 6th Mo. (Aug.), 1661.

Though separated and far off from one another, Crisp is dear and near to the writer, who would rejoice to have a line or two before he goes into the north, which will be ere long. His love is much enlarged towards Friends there, since their imprisonment, and his desire is to visit them. His sister Jane dearly salutes Crisp.

89. Letter from Penn to Crisp, not dated, but written from Worminghurst, not long before the 1st September, 1682. (Clarkson's "Life of Penn," Lond., 1813. Vol. i., p. 328.)

His fellowship in the Gospel of Peace is more dear to him than all the treasures of the world. They need not say much to each other, his love at parting dwells with him. He has also his letter. There is room for much work in that ground [Pennsylvania]. Does not believe God's Providenc had run that way towards him, but that he had an heavenly end and service in it. C. Taylor, J. Harrison, and others salute him. His love is to Friends, especially in Holland, Colchester, and London. This goes by his agent and kinsman [James Harrisson]. His came yesterday by hand by J. Massy.

90. Letter from Joseph Fuce to Crisp, London, 30th of 1st Mo. (March), 1664.

---

* I am inclined to think this letter is addressed to the above, and not another John Swinton, although I have as yet found no direct evidence that he was ever in Essex, or imprisoned in Newgate. [ED.]

He has received the especial and efficacious lines of the 22nd of 1st Mo, '64, and is glad to hear Crisp has been in the country [? Holland] with Thomas Beale, which must have refreshed Friends there after their long sufferings. Would much like to have seen J. Crook, and testified against his paper and his deeds. Is sorry he should lodge at the houses of some, rather than with others, sounder, though not so great in the outward. Felt also a godly jealousy over Giles Barnardiston, by his lodging at Michael J. and I. Peningtons. Concerning C. B., he has not heard wherefore they removed him from St. Albans to the Tower, but the common saying is it was for treasonable words. He hath not behaved well since being at the Tower, hath borrowed money, and is too shallow even to hide his deceit from his own party ; they speake of his release shortly.

Crisp may have heard of the stir among the prentices last 7th, 1st, and 2nd days [Saturday, Sunday, and Monday]. They rose about two boys condemned to stand in the pillory, and be whipt in Cheapside, for resisting their master, who, through cruelty, had provoked them. The prentices pulled down the pillory. When the trained bands were raised upon them, a new one was set up, and ,by armed force, the youths set in it. Brown is counted the chief instigator in the business, and the boys are desperately set against him. There is a stir about the Triennial Bill, and something they say is done, but he has not learned what, for he goes little abroad, by reason of weakness. The assizes at Durham are not for two or three months ; there is a report of J. H. [John Harwood] that he is like to go back to the Church of England, but H. N. [Humphrey Norton] is, as formerly, a prisoner. The news concerning J. P. [John Philley] in Germany is sad, and is further confirmed by a copy of a letter from his interpreter, to Benjamin Furly ; to outward appearance, he is like to suffer death. They must leave the thing to the Lord, who can set the soul of the righteous in peace. Some words have been lately spoken, as if the King had presented a Bill to Parliament against meetings, but little certain is known. Thinks next week to go into the country, southwards, to repair his health. The sessions are to be at Yarmouth, the 6th of 2nd month ; has endeavoured much for Will. and the other Friends enlargement, and the liberty they did have was through a lords letter to the bailiffs.

JOSEPH FUCE was a native of Surrey. As a young man, he entered the parliamentary army, and was serving as an ensign, at Lynn, when Fox visited that place in 1655. (*Journal*, ed. 1765, p, 143.) After joining Friends he travelled in the southern counties, and was often in prison. Once, being arrested at a meeting by order of the mayor of Arundel, he was sent to Portsmouth, to be shipped for Jamaica with convicts, but being neither charged, nor convicted, of any crime, he was released. He was afterwards imprisoned in Sandown, and Dover castles, and in Ipswich jail, and the White Lion prison, Southwark. He died at Kingston on the 9th of October, 1669. (Barclay's Letters, Lond., 1841, Ellis Hookes to George Fox, LXIII. p. 168.)

GILES BARNARDISTON, mentioned in the above letter, was born at Clare, Suffolk, in 1624, a member of the ancient family of Barnardiston of that county. He received an excellent education, and proceeded to Cambridge, where he graduated in due course, and prepared to enter the church, but on a living being presented to him, he became " conscious of wanting that internal purity and spiritual wisdom which he conceived essential qualifications for gospel ministers." (Gough, vol ii. p. 549.) Upon the commencement of the civil war, Giles Barnardiston received a commission as Colonel in the army, which, however, he soon resigned, and retired to Wormingford Lodge, Essex, where he devoted himself to a life of pious seeking. About 1661, feeling curious about the quakers, he invited George Fox, junior, then in Colchester, and George Weatherly, of Colchester, whom Crisp calls his cousin, to his house. The meeting resulted in Barnardiston joining the quakers, who were at that time undergoing violent persecutions, in Colchester and elsewhere. Of this the new convert received his full share. Besse (vol. i. p. 200) records that he " willingly bore his part of this storm of persecution, in the hottest of which he constantly attended religious meetings, and undauntedly hazarded his life for his testimony."

In 1669 he went back to his birthplace, Clare, to live, and the following year was severely distrained upon under a warrant granted by Gervas Elways, a magistrate, for meeting in defiance of the Conventicle Act. He became a minister in the Society, and travelled for the gospel throughout England and Holland.

Returning from London he was taken ill at Chelmsford, and died there the 11th January, 1681, aged about fifty-six.

91. Sarah Warner's dreams, 1st of 9th Mo. (Nov.), 1684.

She fell asleep and dreamed she was in an alehouse, where were twelve men, for whom she was dressing meat. Was concerned to find herself there, but concluded she was lent to help them. So she awoke, and sleeping soon after, dreamed she went to the same house as a visitor, it being London, and she about her trade. The house, she reckoned, stood at the corner of Houndsditch. Great was her fright to find the men all lying, not dead, but bleeding, round about the door, soldiers on guard behind, and a boisterous man who met her, saying no citizen could go in or out. She stood in terror, not being able to put a foot to the ground, for the bodies of men. Porters and carmen came to open the gates, but their enemies took their things to arm themselves with. She thought to get from gate to gate, and so at last out of the city, but a voice said, " All the gates are shut, there is no deliverance." As she passed on in terror, there was no man citizen to be seen, but all were hid in their houses, while the women, with faces white as dead corpses, wrung their hands, and cried, " We are all undone." Then she cried to the Lord, but his face was hid from her. As she walked on through this miserable city, she could not see one quaker ; all, save herself, in this doomed city were in a place of safety. At length she reached Cheapside, and when she looked for the stocks market, behold, all the stalls were flung down, the herbs and fruits trodden under foot, and the women at the stalls were all like dead corpses. Then, she argued to herself, these people slay no women, yet as she spoke, she saw one take a little boy out of his mother's arms, and slay them both together. At this, her terror reached its height, and she awoke, with a prophetic sense that she would one day see these things really acted, and find herself forsaken of the Lord.

Three months after, she dreamed again that she was at a great meeting, where were many Friends, and some of the ministry, when the officers came and took her away. She was brought to trial, and for not yielding to their will, committed to prison until the day of execution. Multitudes came to see her die, her mother, Aunt Tiler, sister, and Justice Fox. The crowd was troubled that she should die, and begged Justice Fox to save her life, as he had previously showed her kindness, but he sternly replied he must see her dead before he left the place. The executioner stood at her right hand, her relations at her left. She spoke much to the people, but what she said passed out of her mind. She was unwilling to die, could she have lived clear in the sight of God, but she saw no way unless she promised to forsake the truth. She chose death rather, and cheerfully went to put off her linen, to give to her relations, each of them some. The executioner became importunate to know if she was ready, but being loath to die, she delayed him, still hoping to be at the last spared. At last she was made willing, and turning to her weeping sister, bade her be faithful, and so bidding farewell to all, looked to the executioner, who placed the halter about her neck.

Slowly the pains of death overcame her, and as she waked, she knew her life had ebbed away.

Oft-times she is considering what the meaning of these dreams should be, and is ready to believe they are sent for a warning that she should be in readiness against the testings which doe appear likely to come to pass, on all professing the truth. Yet there is comfort to her in the thought that, as she was forsaken in the former, so in the latter dream, she was strengthened to stand faithful unto death.

92.   Several pages of MSS. of books printed by Crisp, endorsed by him as such.

93.   See Furly. No 10.

94.   Rough and much corrected copy, in G. Whitehead's writing, of the answer to the appeal of Friends in Holland, for advice as to giving notice of marriages, to the magistrates. Addressed to Peter Hendricks, Jan Roelofs, B. Furly, and Jan Claus, dated London, 27th of 6th Mo. (Aug.), 1683, and signed by George Fox, Alexander Parker, George Whitehead, James Parke, Wm. Gibson, Thos. Robertson, John Vaughton.

See Nos. 1, 10, and 83, which relate to the same subject.

95. See Hendricks, No. 18.

96. An Epistle . . . concerning the decease of our faithful brother George Fox, from our second day's morning meeting in London the 26th of the 11th Mo., 1690 (Feb., 1691), signed by twenty-one Friends, headed by Crisp. Printed, 4 pp. fscap. fol.

97. Directions to collect matter for a General History of the Entrance and Progress of Truth in this Age, by way of annals. Broadside.

98. Letter from Crisp to John Philley, dated London, 23rd of 9th Mo. (Nov.), 1669.

If the weight of disservice he has done to truth, did rest upon him, he would forbear the spirit that led him thereto. Is not his dreams and falsehoods, whereby he has stopt the progress of truth in .Germany, enough, but he must now scribble to the Duke of Buckingham. Leave flattering and dissimulation, and mind to know his own spirit, for his work stinks in the nostrils of them that have a true savour of truth He has often been warned, now let him seek true judgment in himself in which he would know the writer to be his friend.

JOHN PHILLEY was a schoolmaster at Dover, who was imprisoned there in 1670, for teaching without a license from the Bishop. In 1662, with William Moore, he visited Germany, and from thence went on to Austria and Hungary, where they were for a long time imprisoned by the Inquisition, and at last effected a most extraordinary escape, related in "The Narrative of John Philley and William Moore," Friends' Library, Vol. IV., Philadelphia, 1840, &c.

99. See Hendricks, No. 18.

100. See Bradford, No. 16.

101. Letter from John Whitehead to Crisp, from Lincolne Castle, the 13th day of the 6th Mo. (Aug.), 1662. (John Kendall's "Letters from I. Penington and Miscellaneous Letters," London, 1769, p. 93.)

Surely a day is coming, when the tender lambs shall lie down in safety in the virtue of endless love. Touching Friends in those parts, and the county of York, he has not much to communicate, save that he was released out of that prison, by Judge Twisden, for about five weeks in all, and had a good service, mostly in York, and Lincolnshire, but he also touched upon the county of Durham. Left Friends more clean, fresh, lively, and virtuous than he had known them since the first ingathering, and to his comfort, he daily hears they continue so. They are but eight prisoners, four for tithes, himself, and other three, because they cannot swear. The judge refused to hear their case, though they were committed to the assize, he supposes lest they should have cleared themselves from the manifold false assertions contained in the charge, so they are committed till next sessions at Durham. Hears the rest of Friends are released, and moderately fined, upon the New Act, at York, where eighty were released and about fifty-five left in prison, some for tithes, and some indited upon the New Act, but not tried. Three, to wit John Leavens, Samuel Poole, and Cristopher Poole, the Judge (though in the rest of his proceedings moderate) did run into a premunire, and gave sentence of imprisonment for life, with loss of all their lands and goods. Many meetings in Yorkshire have, since the general imprisonment, remained undisturbed, among such Holderness and Hull. Marmaduke Storr, his wife, and divers other Holderness Friends have been lately to visit him, and desire their love. Also his dear wife, who is sick at present. His heart is enlarged to all Friends that way, at Colchester, and at Coggeshall, salute them as there is opportunity. Received one letter from Crisp, when in prison there before, forbore to answer, not knowing how to send. If this comes to Crisps hand, let him know. A letter may be sent to Richard Davies in London, who can send to Lincoln every week, so shall he be encouraged to write again.

JOHN WHITEHEAD was born at Owstwick in Holderness, East Riding of Yorks, and afterwards lived at Bale, Lincolnshire. He seems to have been an especial object of persecution from the priests and magistrates, and was continually in prison at Lincoln, Hull, Spalding, and Newgate, for holding meetings, and preaching. He was a copious writer, and his collected works were published, London, 1704, 8vo. He died 29th September, 1696, at his house at Fiskerton, Lincoln, and was buried in the Friends' Cemetery, at Lincoln. (Smith's Catalogue, and Chalkley's Life of J.W., London, 1852, 12mo.)

102. See Rofe, No. 49.

103. A letter dated London, 30th of 3rd Mo. (May), 1683, signed by Geo. Fox, James Parke, Robert Lodge, Leonard Fell, and Steven Crisp, to two Friends, not named, offering advice on the marriage of cousins.

104. See Furly, No. 10.

105. See Lodge, No. 26.

106. The award of Steven Crisp, of Colchester, between Henry Halls, of Shotsham, and Elizabeth Halls, of Saxlingham, both in the county of Norfolk, dated this fifth day of the sixth Month, called August, 1669.

107. Letter from Josiah Coale to Crisp, dated " neare Gilford in Sury, this 12th of 9th Mo. [Nov.], 1664."

Most dearly salutes Crisp, his wife, and the rest of the faithful in that
place [Colchester]. Truly Crisps share is larger than many, to bear the
burdens of the weak, and sometimes of the wicked also, and of false
brethren, which is the worst of all. May they both, by the power
working in their hearts, rule and reign over the world. Is now upon a
journey to Cornwall, to visit Friends as he is led. Things are quiet in
those parts [Surrey], and Truth prosperous.

JOSIAH COALE was a native of Winterbourne, near Bristol, and was there
convinced by the preaching of John Audland, about 1855. He travelled
much in England, Holland, and the Low Countries with Crisp, as well
as in Barbadoes and Virginia, where he visited the Indians. He was
more than once imprisoned, and finally banished from Maryland. He
wrote, while in gaol at Launceston, Cornwall, 1664, "The Whore un-
vailed, or the Mystery of the Church of Rome explained," published 1667,
and other Tracts and Epistles, published collectively, London (?), 1671,
4to. He also wrote a reply to the famous Ludovic Muggleton. Crisp
was with him when he died, aged thirty-five, in the year 1668.

108. An account of the Estate in Friends' hands, examined and placed in a book, by Thomas Bayles, John Furly,
the elder, and Peter Langley.

"Here followeth an account of the estate in Friends hands ; both of
the Meeting Houses and grounds and yards for Buriall places, and other
houses ; how they came into their hands, to witt by gifts and purchases,
and of the severall buildings erected at their cost. As also the severall
settlements, the names of the Trustees, and their perticuler services :
also other of the solemn promises and agreements of the Trustees, with
their Friends and Brethren, to performe and discharge according to the
trust committed unto them ; which is done that those Friends which
shall have occasion to looke them over, may do it more readily, than as
they stand recorded in the booke of Friends, in parts and pieces in
seaverall places.

" The trust committed to the Trustees was to secure the estate and
titles, against the envy of informers and other evill minded men, which
in those daies, frequently lay in wait to make a prey of us and what we
had. . . Thus was and is this estate settled to remaine according to
the first settlement, to be an estate for ever, absolutely without any condition, redemption, or revocation, and is left to Friends that shall afterwards, through the grace of God, come into the fellowship with the
faithful in Christ Jesus, to take care and see it be preserved in the
service for which it was at first raised, which was for the benefit of
meetings, the buriall of the dead, and that the poor (whose the houses
of the Chappell are, as is shewd in this Booke in the account of that
estate, being bought with their money given unto them by the Charity
and free disposition of Loveing and faithfull Friends that are now deceased), be distributed and paid unto them as at first was done every

(From the painting engraved by Francis Place.)

JAMES NAYLER.

yeare (as appears by Solomon Freemantels Booke now resting and remaining with the writings of the said estate in Friends box), for the relieving and comforting of honest poore men, women and children, that were then with us, both aged and in necessity.

"It is to be remembered to posterity to be considered what occasion there will be for trustees for the future, seeing that the government is become friendly to us, whereby those informers laying in wait by the statute of Mortmain to seize estates given to charitable uses without License, are worne out. Or if it should be judged needfull to continue them, then to be strict in the choice, and to put in a clause into the Solemn promise and engagement that if any one or more of the Trustees shall at any time deny the meetings, or not frequent them, or be denyed by the said people called Quakers in Colchester, that henceforth they shall ccase from being Trustees, their names be razed out of the booke, and the mens meeting forthwith nominate and chuse others in their stead, as if they or he were actually dead."

1st. The graveyard in Moor Elms Lane, in Buttolphs Parish, the gift of Thomas Bayles, under date 20th of 12th Mo., 1659 (Feb., 1660). Solomon Freemantle, and Steven Crisp, the two surviving trustees, settled it upon six others, by deed bearing date the 24th of 1st Mo., 1686. 2nd. The graveyard in Almshouse Lane, in Nicholas Parish, bought of Ann Stammage, and settled upon trustees 16th of 5th Mo. (July), 1667.

3rd. The three tenements given by Thomas Brabrooke, in James Parish, East St., Colchester, according to his will, dated 23rd of 8th Mo. (Oct.), 1669. 4th. The great Meeting House in Martins Lane, purchased of Thomas Bayles, and by a deed dated 16th of 12th Mo., 1671 (Feb., 1672), settled on trustees, of whom Benjamin Furly was one.

5th. The Chappell houses in St. Helens Lane, and grounds, part of which is a burying place, purchased of Robert Torkington by Steven Crisp, by appointment, under a deed dated 20th of April, 1683, for £405 7s. 6d.

This money was advanced by different Friends, among them £50 by Steven Crisp, or his wife Gertrude, upon which during his life-time 50 shillings per year, was to be paid to Daniel Vanderwall. Upon part of these premises abutting southwards, Gertrude Losvelt (second wife to Steven Crisp) built four dwelling-houses, for widows of poor Friends to live in.

Then follow the agreements of the trustees for the several grounds, houses, and premises ; the clause of the will of Elizabeth Greene, 1666, concerning her gift to poor friends ; the gift of Gyles Sayer, who died in September, 1708, to poor friends ; and the names of those friends empowered to grant burial notes. Among these occur those of Solomon Freemantle, John Furly, Jun., and Steven Crisp. The burial ground in Moor Lane was in use from 1676 to 1682, when that in Almshouse Lane, St. Nicholas parish, was opened, but in the following year, instructions were given to raise £100 for the purchase of a new ground in the Chappell yard. From 1685 all burials took place there.

The meeting-house in St. Helen's Lane had a history of considerable antiquity, its origin being, it is said, a foundation by St. Helen, the mother of the Emperor Constantine. About 1076 it was rebuilt and given to the monastery of St. John, but in the reign of Edward I, John de Colchester founded a chantry in it. It is stated in Wright's "Essex,"

ii. 312, that it was purchased by the Quakers in 1671, but from the above document it appears it was not until twelve years later. In a document preserved at Colchester, " St. Helen's Chapel, formerly demolished, in the parish of St. Nicholas, is registered as a meeting-house for Quakers, at the visitation of the Rev. William Beveridge, D.D., Archdeacon of Colchester, dated 2nd of May, 1701." It continued to be thus used until the acquisition of another house in 1801, when it was used for a public library, and afterwards as a school for boys.

109. James Nayler, his Psalm of Thanksgiving, published by him, after his fall, 1659. Broadside, printed and sold by the assigns of J. Sowle, at the Bible, in George Yard, Lombard Street, 1723.

The history of JAMES NAYLER, and his notorious trial, with its disproportionate sentence, is too universally known to be more than outlined here. His assumption of the person and character of the Messiah, to early pictures of whom, it is said, he bore a facial resemblance, and his strange rehearsal of Christ's triumphal entry into Jerusalem, re-enacted in the streets of Bristol, are known wherever quaker history is known. These acts formed the culminating point of the wild extravagances into which some of George Fox's early disciples were led, but with which the severest critic cannot but dissociate Fox himself.

Born at Anderslow, in Yorkshire, the son of one " Goodman Nayler, so called in the country," James Nayler grew up a pious husbandman. He served eight or nine years in the parliamentary army, became a quartermaster in Lambert's troop, and was a member of an Independent church at Weedchurch. He married early, and settled at Wakefield, to which town Fox came to preach in 1650. Nayler soon joined forces with him, and the next year, while travelling together, they were arrested for preaching at Walney Island, in Lancashire. Nayler was committed to Appleby gaol, where he had for his fellow-prisoners Howgill and Burrough. He remained in prison five months, and during the time, wrote in his defence, " Truth cleared from Scandal," 1654, and many other tracts. Shortly after being released, Nayler joined Howgill and Burrough, who, by their preaching, were attracting the larger part of the religious life of London. Nayler's ministry became extremely popular. " Many from the Court went to hear him," Sir Harry Vane, titled ladies, and officers of the army. His eloquence was praised, and by the adulation offered, his mind temporarily lost its balance. Up to that time, he had enjoyed the entire confidence of the Society, who therefore became, in the eyes of the general public, inculpated in acts which when analysed, resolved themselves into the temporary insanity of Nayler, and the religious excitement of three women, and one man.

The trial of Nayler took place before the House of Commons, from Dec. 5th, 1656. Thurloe, writing to Henry Cromwell, 16th Dec., says :— " The Parliament hath done nothing this ten days but dispute whether James Nayler shall be put to death for blasphemy. They are much divided in their opinions ; it is probable his life may be spared." The motion was in fact lost by fourteen votes (96-82), and Nayler's sentence, crueller than death, was carried out in all its hideous details.

During his imprisonment, and after his release, Nayler manifested the most unfeigned repentance for his former follies, and was restored to unity with his Friends. His last " Testimony," delivered about two hours before his death, a passage of great beauty, beginning " There is a spirit which I feel, that delighteth to do no evil," shows a gentle, humble spirit, in marked contrast to his former career, and is universally known. He died at Holm, near King's Ripton, Huntingdonshire, in the end of October, 1660, aged about fourty-four.

The illustration is from the portrait of Nayler, painted and engraved by Francis Place (d. 1728), second to practise the art of mezzotinting introduced into England by Prince Rupert. It was afterwards engraved by Preston and Grave, both of whom accentuated its strongly marked characteristics, which in the print published 1823, amount to positive ugliness.

110. See Rous. No. 86.

111. Robert Barrow to Geo. Whitehead, and Crisp, addressed to the former, at his house, near Devonshire Square, dated from Kingswell, 4 miles from Aberdeen, in Scotland, the 15th of 11th Month, 1691 (Jan., 1692).

He, with many more, is truly sensible of their daily concern in truths affairs. Used formerly to write to G. Ff., who has finished his day in heavenly renown. Writes now to them, believing they have a universall eye over all the churches in Europe and America. This is to tell them he has visited Friends meetings throughout the most part of that nation, and found them generally in good order. About Aberdeen, and northwards of it, divers are of late convinced, the name of an Englishman is famous among them. Proposes to return south to Edinburgh, thence to Glasgow, where the city rabble entertained him very kindly last time, throwing dirt and stones. Since then, Robert Wardell, of Sunderland, in Bishoprick [See No. 122], and James Halliday of Northumberland, were there, and haled out of their meeting house by the officers, who put seventeen in prison, keeping some twelve days without a mittimus. They also took the forms and seats, and will not restore them ; the Provost saith they shall not meet there while he has power to prevent. These things have been laid before the Kings Council at Edinburgh (it having taken place last 9th Mo.) They are the most rigidest sort of Presbyterians, called Cameronians, or mountain men, and so hot and seared about their covenant that other parts of the body of Scotland hold them in contempt. In all other places, the inhabitants and soldiers are moderate towards Friends. Having opportunity to send this by a friends son, who is going to be an apprentice, he further lets them know he thinks of visiting Ireland, and will take shipping from the west of Scotland. The lad, who is to goe to John Dawsons, comes of good parents, his father being Andrew Jaffryes [Jaffray], the most noted man among Friends, both in testimony, and in church care, and government. Would like some oversight taken of him for his parents sake. Gilbert Mollison brought the bargain to pass, and can give further account of the matter.

Some portion of this letter is printed in Jaffray's "Diary," Lond., 1834, p. 474. It is dated from Kingswell, the seat of Andrew Jaffray, Provost of Aberdeen, one of the Scottish Commissioners to Charles II., and a member of Cromwell's Parliament. Gilbert Molleson was a magistrate, of Aberdeen, whose wife Margaret early joined the quakers. Their daughter Christian became the wife of Barclay, the Apologist.

ROBERT BARROW was born in Lancashire. He was early convinced of quakerism, and became a minister, travelling extensively in England, Scotland, Wales, and Ireland. He was many times imprisoned. He married Margaret Bisbrown, of Arnside. In 1694 he went to America, and the West Indies, on a gospel visit, and in travelling from the latter to Pennsylvania, he, with his companions, was shipwrecked in the Gulf of Florida, and fell into the hands of Indians, by whom they were badly treated, and stripped of their clothing. Barrow's age and infirmity were unable to stand against the long and tedious journey to Pennsylvania. Three days after arriving there he died, on 6th April, 1697, and was buried in the cemetery at Philadelphia. ("God's Protecting Providence," by Jonathan Dickenson, Philadelphia and London, 1700, 12mo, and many subsequent editions.")

113.   Letter from R. R. to Crisp.   No date.

Old Chaucer, whose manuscript was shown to the writer by his correspondent, gave them such an occasion of discourse upon language, that he came away with the book under his arm, which gave him the more time to peruse it. Finds he can understand it well, which at a like distance of time, Polybius testifies the best antiquaries could not the Latin. Three hundred years after the treaty between the Romans and Carthaginians, the former could not read it by reason of the changes in the language. That on the other side is writ in Latin, to be more emphatical. He shewed it, twenty-four years ago, to Hammod, of Newcastle, commissioned by the Parliament to examine all ministers and schoolmasters. At that time, the writer was master of a free school. The verses are no conceit, but well digested. It does some good, but also more hurt. Quere whether the common prayer, and professors meetings do not likewise. If one of a thousand have a mind to travel he should not allure g.g.g. to go along with him without cause. Dutch may be sooner gained than Latin, and with more service ; also French, Spanish, and Italian, in the time spent over it, yea, the substance of most necessary learning. A treatise might be writ hereof.

The Latin verses, entitled *De Etymologiâ Latinâ aborigine, cur a latendo dicto* follow.

114. Orders signed by Wiardi Huberts, D. Sec. for the banishment of Cornelis Andreas, his wife, Hester Jansen, with other quakers, from the city of Embden, dated the 21st July, and 4th August, 1674.

115. Copied extracts from Charles IX., Emanuel Demeirus, the Archduke Methsias, Marier's Hist, fol., 1561, Johannem Macronam, 1604, concerning peace in matters of religion.

116. Two numbers of *The London Gazette*, Mon. to Thurs., Mar. 3rd, and Thurs. to Mon., Mar. 7th, 1686, containing the King's Proclamation of Toleration to Presbyterians, Quakers, Papists, and others, and the Deputy of Ireland, Tyrconnell's, declaration of the same, as relating to Ireland.

117. Paper of George Whitehead's (copy).

118. Ditto, headed "These disorders concerning marriages, the Testimony of Truth stands against," signed G. W.

119. Unsigned letter to Crisp, dated Ennemessike (Maryland), 5th of 2nd Mo. (April), (16)64.

The writers soul is refreshed with the wine of the only vine. Crisps salutation, sent by W. Harward's maid, was received. Great conflicts, within and without, have been endured since leaving England, amongst relations bitter against the truth. Many Friends have been whipped in New England, both before and since the writer was there, likewise in Virginia, but in Maryland province, they have liberty yet. Direct to the care of Thomas Thurston, or to Samuel Groome, master of a vessel, who will deliver them safe.

120. Copy of an Epistle from the Quarterly Meeting held at Colchester, 8th of 4th Mo. (June), 1691.

121. Preface to a book, commencing "Christian Reader,

whereas in these latter days," and signed " A lover of thy soul, whoever thou art, whether friend or enemy. S. C."*

122. Letter from Robert Wardell, to Crisp, with particulars of Robt. Lodge, and John Burnyeat, deceased, dated Sunderland, 1st of 11th Mo., [16]90, (Jan., 1691), and addressed to Crisp, at Wm. Crouch's, in Crown Court, Gracechurch Street.

His first acquaintance with them was in Ireland, about the year [16]57, at a meeting at Bellarbutt, in the county of Cavan. A large body of soldiers, horse and foot, came to break it up, and drove the Friends out of the town. Burnyeat and Lodge travelled many weary steps, by day and night, on foot, for the settlement of meetings, particularly a large one, at or near Moate, in the county of Meath. The city of Londonderry did great despite to them. May more such faithful labourers be raised. Many are the exercises of mind he has had with dear Robt. Lodge. One vision in particular he relates, and describes how he saw him sitting in a great meeting, watered with a heavenly fountain. This, which he calls " A Lively Emblem," the writer saw, on the night of the 16th of the 9th Mo. (Nov.), 1690.

JOHN BURNYEAT was born at Crabtreebeck, in the parish of Loweswater, Cumberland, in the year 1632. " His parents were of good repute, and his education was according to his parentage." He seems to have had early religious impressions, and when he was about twenty, George Fox came into Cumberland to preach, whereby, he says, he was "directed unto the true light." After Fox had departed, Burnyeat and some others, like minded, met often together, as "the Lord's messengers" had exhorted them. Thus they established a congregation, who "wanted [i.e., lacked] not a teacher, nor true divine instruction, though we had left the hireling priests, and other high-flown notionists." Until 1657 he remained at home, "following his outward calling" and paying occasional visits to those in prison for conscience. He then felt called to go and testify openly against the priests, and their manner of conducting worship for hire. After boldly, and with impunity, haranguing Warwick of Aspatria, Fogoe of Lorton, and others, he was arrested, when defending the Friends from an attack made upon them by "Priest Denton" of Briggham. The people, he says, did beat him "with their bibles and staves all along the house and out of the church yard," when the priest commanded a constable to arrest him, and carry him next day to Lancelot Fletcher, of Talantyre, who ordered a warrant to be writ to convey him to Carlisle gaol. Here he remained twenty-three

---

* I have not succeeded in finding this in print. ED.

weeks. In October, 1658, Burnyeat set out for Scotland, where he travelled for three months, going as far north as Aberdeen. In May, 1659,° he sailed from Whitehaven for Ireland, and landed at Donaghadee in Ulster. Travelling on foot, he visited the whole of that province, Dublin, Kilkenny, Munster, Wexford, Carlow, and Mountmellick. At Lurgan, on his way north, he met Robert Lodge, a Yorkshireman, with whom he afterwards spent many days. They united their forces, and spent about twelve months labouring together, their mission chiefly being to preach against "hireling priests." They were several times imprisoned, in Armagh, Dublin, and Cork, and in September, 1660, they sailed from Carrickfergus for England.

Burnyeat remained at "his outward calling" until September, 1660, when he went up to London to acquaint George Fox and others of the elders, with the "weight" that was upon him to go to America. In his account, he says that he consulted with Fox, Burrough, and Hubberthorn, for he "loved to have the counsel and countenance of his elder brethren." Returning home through Yorkshire, he visited some Friends in prison at Ripon, and here the Mayor and some of the Aldermen sought hard to get him also imprisoned. Failing to obtain from him answers to the questions, when last he was at church, or took the sacrament, the Mayor reached for a book, and asked him to take the oath of allegiance and supremacy. Burnyeat's reply "Not in contempt to the king or his authority, but in obedience to Christ's command, I cannot swear," infuriated the Mayor, who commanded the clerk to write a mittimus, and committed him to prison. There he was kept fourteen weeks, and every day he was a fresh and continual annoyance to the authorities. For just beneath the prison windows was a bowling alley, where several of the magistrates and others amused themselves at their games. Now since the coming of John Burnyeat, he had, as he says, "exhorted and prayed with the [prisoners] once every day," and the sound of these devout quakers at their prayers, seemed entirely out of harmony with the shouts of the players, and the rolling of the balls. They then procured his separation from the other prisoners, and confined him in a little dark dungeon, where he was at one time seven days and nights. As soon as he was released, he returned to Cumberland, and remained at home, with occasional visits into Yorkshire and Durham.

In the early part of the summer of 1664, Burnyeat crossed over to

---

° After a lapse of more than thirty years, a mistake of two years is easily excused on the part of the writer, who says above "about the year 1657.'

Ireland, and in September, sailed from Galway for Barbadoes, arriving there after a passage of seven weeks and two days. Three or four months were spent by him in the island, where he found the influence of John Perrot had caused many to drift away from the earlier traditions. He then proceeded to Maryland for the following summer, and to Virginia for the winter, where he also found Perrot's influence strong. He having persuaded the Friends that meeting together was a form, they had abandoned their gatherings.

In June 1666, Burnyeat arrived at New York, and proceeded leisurely through Rhode Island, New England, Sandwich, etc., to Boston. After which he went to Long Island, and back again to Rhode Island, where he stayed some time, " for there was no going off the Island unto the main, in the winter, the snow was so deep." He spent the next summer in Barbadoes, where he says he had " blessed and comfortable service among Friends," and in September, 1667, he sailed for Bristol. The length of the voyage is forcibly brought before us, when we read in his journal:—" After we had been ten weeks at the Sea, except one day or two, being beat off the coast with an easterly storm, and kept out at sea in a great tempest, for the most part of two weeks, at last we got into Milford Haven, and there I landed, about the 29th of the 9th Month (Nov.) 1667." John Burnyeat remained in Wales for some time, visiting the meetings, and then went up to London, afterwards meeting George Fox in Surrey. Continual visits to London, and all parts of England and Ireland, occupied him until about July 1670, when he was again " moved " to go to Barbadoes. His companion, William Simpson, after reaching the Island, took fever, which was very prevalent there, and died in six days. Burnyeat continued his service alone, and then proceeded to New York, Rhode Island, Maryland, and all the numerous places he had before visited, in company with Daniel Gould, of Rhode Island. To Virginia also he went, and urged upon the members there, the establishment of a "mens meeting," or meeting for business. Taking boat again for Maryland, he appointed a meeting at West River for all the Friends in the province. George Fox, Robert Widders (or Withers) and several other English Friends arrived from Barbadoes, and a very large meeting was held, which lasted for several days. Burnyeat's account of the succeeding travels through the woods, and to the Indian settlements is extremely interesting, but too long to quote here. Burnyeat proceeded to Boston, where Priest Thatcher stirred up the magistrates, and some Friends were arrested, including John Stubbs and James Lancaster, who were sent out of the country. At Hampton, not far from

Salem, the priest, Seaborn Cotton,[c] also endeavoured to stir up persecution against them.

On returning to Rhode Island, the Friends received a challenge from Roger Williams, of Providence, with fourteen propositions to dispute. Three days were spent in discussion, before a "large congregation,' some account of which Burnyeat says "is printed in a book entituled, *A New England Fire-brand Quenched.* 1679 [London 4to], to which I refer the reader." William Edmondson was present at the discussion. After this Burnyeat met with much opposition at Hartford, in Connecticut, the elders of the churches being greatly alarmed lest the young people should be converted. One of the elders, the landlord of the inn, took away the candle that he might not see to read the Scriptures.

Burnyeat returned to Ireland in May 1673, and travelled continuously in that country, going afterwards to London, and then to the West of England, and Wales. For preaching at Devonshire House, he was fined £20 by Sir Samuel Starling, Mayor, and a fortnight later, committed to Newgate for the same cause. While travelling in Wales, his mare, saddle, and bridle, valued at £8, were taken from him, and he was left to proceed on foot. He was also many times imprisoned in the Marshalsea prison, Dublin.

John Burnyeat married an Irish Friend in 1683, and settled in Dublin, Her name does not appear. She died in 1688, leaving one son. He continued his incessant travels until only twelve days before his death, when a sudden fever attacked him. He died in Dublin, 11th Sept., 1690, in the fifty-ninth year of his age, and was buried at New Garden.

He seems to have been universally loved, and is described in the "Testimonies," as of "innocent deportment and blameless conversation, which preached wherever he came, moderate in meat, drink, and apparel. And in all his Travels, into whose house he entred, he was content with what things were set before him, were they never so mean; which was great satisfaction to many poor honest Friends among whom his lot was cast." ("The Truth exalted in the Writings of that eminent and faithful servant of Christ, John Burnyeat, collected into this ensuing volume, as a Memorial to his faithful labours in and for the Truth." London, 1691.)

123. An Epistle from the meeting of men Friends in Colchester, 4th of 12th Mo., 1694 (Feb., 1695).

124 and 127. Letters from John Hallaway to Crisp, dated the 7th of 10th Mo. (Dec.), and 6th of 12th Mo. (Feb.), 1666.

It is seven years since his heart was set to seek the Lord, and seeing Friends in the street, he would willingly have had fellowship with them, but dared not to speak. After a time came to the meeting. G. W[hitehead] was there, it was five years before. Also went to a meeting held by T. G. at Boxstead. Relates various visions. In the 2nd letter, mentions one in which he saw John Rofe in East Street [Colchester], and immediately began digging a grave for him, he having heard that this Friend and G. E. were both taken with "the sickness."

---

* Seaborn Cotton was son of John Cotton (1585-1632), one of the first ministers at Boston.

125. A paper of George Fox's (copy).

126. Letter from Robert Morffe to Crisp, dated Colchester, 26th of 4th Mo. (June), 1686.

It has been often his mind to shew certain loose papers, and ask Crisps counsel, as a father in the truth. Cannot put it up any longer, but must bring it forth. Keep them secret until they speak together Tis no vain-glorious conceit to teach others, who needs to be taught himself, but it grieves him to see the blind lead the blind, and, like the Samaritans, worship they know not what. Desires only to leave the manuscript to his children, being not perfected, but a rough draught, wherein he stammers as a child, and cannot express in words what he inwardly conceives, but presses forward, for in the light shall they see light.*

128. see Hendricks, No. 18.

129. Letter from Lewis Morris to Crisp, dated Barbadoes, the 18th of 12th Mo. 1670 (Feb., 1671), and addressed "to be left with Wm. Crouch, upholder†, at Devonshire House without Bishopps Gate, London."

Received Crisps by the hand of John Rous, from Hamborrow [Hamburgh]. It was read at the mens meeting, where John Burnyeat and William Simson were present. The latter is lately departed out of the body. Since his coming from England, has visited the western parts of New England, where are many Friends, who are refreshed by messengers of the Lord. Those whose building is on the Rock of Ages, need not fear the storm that's coming. Love to William Crouch and his wife, at whose house he hopes this may find his friend.

130. Letter from Katherine Johnson to Crisp, no date or place, probably sent by hand.

Is planted in a vineyard, among tender plants, the waters of Shiloh make glad her heart. Hopes to hear from Crisp. Richard Birds and his wifes love to him.

131 and 132. see Claus, No. 19.

133. Letter from John Higgins to Crisp, dated Amsterdam, 20th of 9th Mo. (Nov.), 1663.

His heart is open to his friend, and to all fellow prisoners suffering with him. The glory of nations and kingdoms is not to be paralleled with the lot of their inheritance. The opportunity of going to Holland presented itself to him in London. He safely reached Rotterdam, where he stayed three weeks, and thence went to Leyden, and had a meeting with Friends. Many enquire for Crisp, probably Peter [Hendricks] and himself will translate a piece of his letter into Dutch for them

---

* The enclosure does not appear. † Upholsterer.

Has seen John Coghen once at his fathers house.   Adrian [Losevelt] is as he was, they have left the Vish-steege, and taken a house about five or six hundred guilders a year rent.   Annekin is now alone with her maids, William [Caton]s imprisonment she takes pretty patiently. Peter [Hendricks], Cornelius [Roeloffs], and Judith [Zinspenning] all send their love.   The Friends are all well, though the sickness called the plague is much at Amsterdam.   Love to Crisps wife, John Furly, T. Bayles, G. Witherly, G[iles] Barnardiston, William and Mary Havens, Solomon [Freemantel] and his wife, and her father and mother, Giles Toyspell, and the rest of good friends.

134—142.   Nine letters from Wm. Caton to Crisp.

138.   Amsterdam, 27th of 3rd Mo. (May), 1662.

Has been to Moort, Rotterdam, Leyden, and Haarlem. A declining spirit seems upon Friends in these places. At Rotterdam, only three men at Meeting besides Benjamin [Furly], wife and maid. Furly was very busie, having bought a house and fine large garden outside the Poorts.° At Leyden a man named Hartigfelt, whose estate was worth tons of gold, objected to his having full libertie, but afterwards came to their house in Amsterdam, where they had a gallant opportunity together. He is very self-denying, and a giver of thousands in a year to the poor. He confessed himself mistaken.   John Coghen is gone again to drink of that bad fountain, the University, to become a doctor. Gertie has been in childbed, but is come up again, her husband is in a bad way. Her love and Annekins, Cornelius, and Peters. Part of the money owing him from Mendlesham is paid. When the rest comes, Steven is to repay John Furly ; though it might have been charged to the public fund, he will feel freer to pay it. Why burden the public, seeing he is able.   It was 10s. disbursed for letters. Judiths son [Sewel the historian] lives with his uncle (a Friend), and learns Latin. He is apt in his learning, but childish in other things. For several mornings there hath been seen a comet star, not much inferior to that seen in the winter. It appears about three and four in the morning. Judgments are threatened to Holland. Their fleet is not yet out, or ready. Many on the men-of-war go by constraint, not willingly.   Remember him to Crisps wife, Ann Furly and her family, to Friends at Coggeshall, Mary Vanderwall, and others at Harwich, and especially to J. Crooke, if he is still prisoner at Ipswich. Might also name Robert Duncon and wife, Sarah and her husband.

JOHN CROOK (1617—1699), was a justice of the peace, and knight of the shire for Bedfordshire. He joined Friends in 1654, and the next year, entertained on his estate near Luton, a large number of the gentry, who came to hear George Fox. A General Meeting, at which "several thousands were present," was held there in 1657. (Fox's "Journal," p. 266, ed. 1765). His arguments against the legality of his imprisonments show him possessed of much legal knowledge. His numerous writings are of sound literary merit. He died at Hertford, and was buried at Sewel, in Bedfordshire.

° Gates.

140. Amsterdam, 9th of 11th Mo. (Jan., 1663).

Friends are glad to hear of his determination to go over; will be gladder when they see him. All is well in Amsterdam. His wifes love, though outwardly unknown. Their sister Gertrude, and her husband, send their love.

136. London, 7th of 12th Mo. (Feb., 1663.)

Joseph Fuce and the writer purpose going that day to Surrey, and so into Sussex. Many in prison have been sick, several have died since their release. Edward Burr[ough] and Samuel Fisher are likely to be continued, notwithstanding the King's order for their release, probably through Browns° instigation. Is sorry he had not the letters Steven detained for him. Has had none from H. Smith. His judgment is for Steven to go shortly to Holland.

137. Yarmouth, 10th of 12th Mo. (Feb., 1664.)

Crisp and his fellow prisoners have been often in his remembrance since their confinement. Though little exercised in bonds, yet he has had his share of suffering. Has heard often from his dear wife, whose strength and patience under their present trial [separation], have made it something easier to him. Knows not how a woman could more refresh her husband, at such a distance, than she has him. Gertry [her sister, afterwards Mrs. Crisp] writes of her husbands reformation. His fellow prisoners love to Crisp and all his fellow prisoners. They are exceeding diligent, and are most of them become good spinners.

135. Altmore, 19th of 3rd Mo. (May), 1664.

They will be glad to hear of his return to Holland two weeks before. Has that day, with Eliz. Cox [who adds a postscript to the letter], held a good meeting. Is going to Haarlem and Leyden. His wife is enjoying of him after that she had even given up hope of seeing his face again. That very day that she had given up hope, was he brought unexpectedly into her house at night, to the gladdening of her heart. John Coghen is weak in body, but preserves his integrity. The sickness increases, and two or three biers may be seen before the door of one house. Judith [Zinspenning]s love. Annekin received a letter from Crisp lately, but understood Edward Feedham, who brought it, was returning the day it came, so commissions him to answer. They were glad to hear the fury of those violent soldiers was mitigated that they did no further harm, also that John Furly was likely to have more liberty, being removed. His love to Giles Cock. If certain are still in prison when Crisp writes to Ipswich, salute them dearly, also Mary Vanderwall, and all at Harwich, Giles Barnardiston, Thomas Bayles, George Weatherly†, and the rest of Friends in bonds. William Tick and his wife, who lived with them, have gone to Barbadoes intending for Virginia, have met with much hardship. Has heard something of George Rofe being drowned. If Crisp has heard the like, let them know.

141. Amsterdam, 1st of 5th Mo. (July), 1664.

---

* Sir Richard Brown (1605-1683), Clerk of the Council to Charles II.

† Crisp's cousin, see his will, App. A.

Dearly salutes Crisp and his fellow prisoners. Received his large and acceptable letter, and has translated passages out of it and others, for the benefit of Friends. Has talked with some of their choicest professors about all kneeling when one prays ; the letters had the effect of exciting the tenderness of the wise in heart. The sickness increases, a hundred more have died that week than in one week before. John Coghen is better, and is going to Rotterdam to study with Isaac Furnerius° to be a doctor. It will not profit him much. Has enquired about the reprinting of the Act ; cannot hear of its having been printed in Holland, at any rate, not in Amsterdam. Has had a book sent from Maryland, of George Rofes, with confirmation of his being drowned in a small boat in a storm. One of the brethren from Hungary has been at his house that day, and gives a sad relation of the misery in his country by reason of the war, and the barbarity of the Tartarians, who are worse than the Turks. The country where the Emperor hath kept his seat is mostly overcome by them, and it is thought that he and his nobles will be forced to flee. Gertie had intended being with him when he wrote, but she is bowed down with the weight of that which unavoidably comes upon her by reason of her husband, who is as he was. Love to John Furly, and desires John Furly, junior, to let him know what he paid for postage of letters to Yarmouth. Judiths and Peters love. Cornelius [Roelof]s children have small pox. Let Edward Plumstead, jun., know that he has received his letter, and delivered the other to J.C. As for the enclosed of Judiths†, if Crisp learn but to understand it, he will for the future understand Dutch letters the better. Love to all Friends in and out of prison.

134. Amsterdam, 11th of 9th Mo. (Nov.), 1664.

It is so long since Crisp was heard of, that his friends are anxious. Bonds and afflictions attend them all, and Friends in Holland are very sensible of the sufferings and trials of those in England. Has been with Barent Roelofs in Friesland. The old man was taken sick, and they returned the sooner. Friends at Altmore, and Leyden are pretty well, at Rotterdam they are scattered. The sickness has abated, last week under 400 died, a thousand has been the usual number. There seems a likelihood of wars between Holland and England. Thanks John Crooke, and Mary Vanderwall for their letters, and replies by this. Greets also Robert Duncon and wife, all at Harwich, and at Colchester. Since writing the letter, he has heard from Benjamin Furly, by which he understands Edward Feedham is come to Rotterdam. Wonders not to have heard from Crisp, by him, and longs for an account of how it is with Friends. His wife will send by the same hand, for Crisp and his fellow-prisoners, two Holland cheeses marked with a P.

142. Amsterdam, 7th of 11th Mo. (Jan., 1665.)

Has translated the substance of Crisps letter for Friends. Wishes he could give as good a report as he receives. Some have scattered and turned backwards, to the saddening of their hearts. J.C.‡ is one. He was moved to speak to him of his absenting himself from meetings, when he complained of Friends formality. What passed is too long to repeat here.

---

* See No. 46. † See No. 33 for the letter enclosed.

‡ [John Coghen, frequently mentioned in these letters.]

He is now gone to Rotterdam, with John Lodge, who is the only one he
will visit, and who has been at great charges in teaching him how to make
combs. At Rotterdam, it is not much better than it was. At Leyden,
and Altmore, little alteration. In Germany, Friends are well, but have
had their goods spoiled. Has sent the large and general Epistle of
P[eter] H[endricks] to Crisp ; let it be read, and the original copy sent to
John Higgins, for him or some friend in London to take a copy, and
then he would desire John to send it to Lancaster, or Kendal. Has
asked John Furly, minimus, for account of his debt for letters to
Yarmouth. Desires to know in the next. One Friends family hath
been visited with sickness, and in two months, eight or nine have been
buried from under his roof. Adrian is as he was, inconstant and fickle,
little as yet seasoned with truth. Gertrude loves the truth, and Friends,
in her very heart, but is bowed down with burdens like she was groaning
under when Crisp was there. She has never forgotten the words he
spake to her. The city is not yet free of the plague. Love to Giles Cock,
Ann Furly, George Wetherley, Gyles Barnadiston, John Crooke, Robert
Duncon, and Mary Vanderwall.

143. Preface by Crisp, beginning "Friendly reader, if
thou art of any sort of people that are reformed in any
measure from the Romish Church," and ending, "know me
by the name of Steven Crisp."°

144. A Tract "To the serious reader. There is nothing in
ye world by which man can be deceived sooner and easier
but by his owne hearte." Four pages.°

145. Another Tract, beginning "The serious reader may
in this paper clearly see thy heart is not good nor honest."
An answer to the preceding. Twelve pages.*

146. Part of the Dutch translation of No. 149, begins at
p. 9, signed J. P., on p. 12 begins "*Zets als een Antwoort op
datgene Hirtwelche jy geschreven hebt in Margine van Pieter
Hendricks boeck, genaent : Den Ernstige betraffinge aen de
Vlaemische Doops-gesinde.*"† Five pages ; signed J.P.‡

147. Pages 3 and 4 of a MS. of Crisp's, about perfection.

148. Title page of James Parke's " Christ Jesus exalted,
and the true light that lightens every man that comes into
the world, born witness to.

"In answer to a dark, confused, and unprofitable paper, subscribed and

---

* These apparently were never published.   † See No. 149.   ‡ James Parke.

sent to us the people of God, called Quakers, by [Jan Kornelisz Knoll], wherein he, in his earthly and sensuall spirit, pleads for outward honner and greetings, after the manner of the contrey, and against our practise who have been led by the Lord God to deny it to all people. Also his soe blasphemously calling the light of Christ imagined light and reason, herein is detested and reproved by the spirit of truth, and according to the testimony and practise of holy men of God mentioned in the Scriptures, to which is added something in answer to what he hath written on the margent of Peter Hendrick's book, that he and all men who are found in such foolish and unprofitable customs and facions of the world may come to see your evill and turn to the light of Christ Jesus and the spirit of God in you, and lead you out of all evill.

"Written by one who loves that which proceeds from, and is wrought in God, but can have no fellowship with unfruitfull works of darknesse, but rather reprove them.—JAMES PARKE."°

II. Kings, iv., 29, "If thou meet any salute him not, if any salute thee answer him not again."

Luke x., 4, "Salute noe man by the way."

James ii., 7.

149. "Something by way of reply to what thou hast written as margent of Pieter Hendricks book called an earnest reproof to ye flemish baptists." (*Een ernstige bestraffinge aen de Vlaemische Doops-gesinde Gemeinte, &c.*, Amsterdam. 1670, 4to. "Collectio," p. 430). Five pages. See No. 146, for Dutch translation of the same.

150. Title page of "An alarm sounded in ye borders of Egypt, which shall be heard in Babylon, and astonish ye Inhabitants of ye polluted Dwelling-places in ye earth, &c., by a servant of God, Steven Crisp."

This book was printed London 1671, reprinted 1672 and 1691, translated into Dutch, *Ein Klang des Allarms.* Amsterdam, 1674.

151. Preface to the same, begins :—

"Courteous Reader, this small treatise comes not forth with the approbation of the learned doctors of our times, neither shall it, I believe, be owned in the academies among the Rabbis, either papal or protestant." Ends "and remaine a friend to thee and all men, S.C."

152. Postscript, "Something further ariseth in my heart which I think good to commemorate, &c.," by Crisp, pp. 1 and 2 only.

---

* This book appears not to have been published in England, but it was translated into Dutch, and published at Amsterdam, 1670, 4to. (See "Collectio," p. 418.)

153. MSS. of Pt. II. of Crisp's Dutch work about the persecution in Friesland. Pt. I. is printed in "Collectio," p. 447, entitled *Een vytroepinge tegens de vervolginge dewelke begonnen is, en voergart door de Regeerders, Predicanten, en Mennisten in Vrieslandt.* "An outcry against the persecution in Friesland, begun and continued by the Magistrates, Ministers, and Mennonites."

The writer proceeds to defend his former book in all he said about the " Menuists " (Mennonites) of Harlingen, and next defends himself against Galenus Abrahams, one of the most noted of the Baptist preachers in Holland, born at Zieriksee, 8th Nov., 1622. He was engaged in a prolonged discussion with Penn and others during the visit to Holland in Sept. and Oct., 1677. After which he relates the history of persecutions in Friesland, especially mentioning the case of Isaac Jacobs, an old man banished from Leeuwarden for ten years, after long imprisonment. Cornelius Roelofs was also imprisoned with him, and wrote an answer to his accusers.

153. A Treatise by Crisp, begins "Manifold are the devices of Satan, and great is the subtlety with which," &c. Twenty-three pages in his own writing.

154. Paper by George Whitehead, signed " A lover of the Seed of God, and a friend to them that follow on to know Him. G. W.," and endorsed " Something to be annexed to the Book of Israels Redemption," &c. Begins " As the following testimony was given forth in the faith of the righteous Seed," &c.

George Whitehead's book " The Seed of Israel's Redemption fully prophecied of (and the Scriptures opened) which now is about to be fulfilled," &c., was published, London, 1659.

155. Six pages in Whitehead's writing, evidently MSS. corrected for press, begins " The difference between the first and second covenants, and the first and second priesthoods," &c.

156. A short relation of the sufferings of Friends at Embden.

This paper contains a sickening account of the petty tyrannies and cruelties imposed upon the people of Embden, by the magistrates. An outline of their sufferings is sketched by Sewel (vol. ii. p. 321), and it is profitless to allude to them further here. It is significant of the spirit of the early Quakers, that no account of these cruelties was ever published in England. Among the Crisp papers at Devonshire House, are several relating to this persecution, but they are all endorsed "Not put in ye English volume, ye case being unknown to us," or "It being judged ye service is now over," or "Ye case altered."

The above illustration represents the winter dress of an Amsterdam Quaker of about 1689. It is copied from one of a series of engravings by Dubourg, for Picart's *Cérémonies et Coutumes Religieuses*, Amster.

1736, tom iv., p. 202. The costume is almost identical with that of a
Mennonite figured in the same work, as also in Maäskamp's *Tableaux
de l'habillements, mœurs et des coutumes*, &c., Amst., 1804. The buttons
form a noteable feature, being continued on either side from the waist
behind. They were manufactured in Holland, and the trade in them
between English and Dutch Friends was, we see from these Letters,
considerable. No. 99 shows a bill from Jan Claus, merchant in Amsterdam, to William Crouch, upholsterer, &c., Gracechurch Street, for 94
gross of buttons, at prices ranging from 33 to 53 stivers° a gross, "sent
unto him according to his order." In No. 56, Simon de Pool says that
the Polish Envoy, having been with him " to hear the inspired Word of
God spoken at the Quakers Meeting, has bought some buttons, and the
money has been given to the poor." Claus, in No. 132, congratulating
John Furly on the birth of a son, "hopes soon to have an order for
buttons," from which it appears the children also wore them.

---

* The Dutch penny, at that time worth of course more than at present.

IMPRISONMENTS AND DISTRAINTS IN ESSEX.

The remaining papers in the Crisp Collection, folios 296—306, under the head of " Sufferings," appear to be pages from an early book, in which such records were kept for transmission to London. From the year 1675, until 1794, a meeting was held weekly in London for the consideration of all reports of imprisonment, fines, &c., forwarded from the country. This was called " The Meeting for Sufferings," and is still held monthly, under the same name. Its original construction was that "at least one Friend of each county be appointed by the Quarterly Meeting thereof, to be in readiness to repair to any of the said meetings at this city, at such times as their urgent occasions or sufferings shall require."

The following entries, though not always dated, are otherwise exact, and afford some curious and interesting information as to the locality and distribution of this people in our own county of Essex; as well as of the family surnames, many of which will still be found in the same villages. There is also some interest, in seeing the nature of the articles in most common use at that time, as well as their estimated value two hundred years ago.

It will here be seen, that there were Friends in almost every district of Essex, from Clacton on Sea to Gestingthorpe, and Castle Hedingham, from Burnham to Hadstock, and from Saffron Walden to Southminster.

IMPRISONED IN ESSEX.

1656.   John Isaac, of Halstead,
        Mary Cook, of Chelmsford,
        John Sewell, of Gestingthorpe,

John Child, of Felstead,

Samuel Skillingham, of Felstead,

Jonathan Bundack,

Steven Hubbersty, and

John Davage, from Dengie-hundred.

1657.

4th Sept.   Mary Bradey, of Felstead,

28th Dec.   Mary Bradey, of Felstead,

John Claiden, of Hadstock.

The above were all imprisoned in Colchester Castle, for offences and periods various.

During the year 1657, there were imprisoned in Colchester Moot Hall, the following Friends, committed chiefly by William Motte, Deputy Recorder, John Vicars being Mayor from Nov. 1656, followed by Nicholas Beacon.

Martha Simmons,

Thomas Shortland,

Steven Crisp,

Edmond Crosse,

Anne Langley (four times),

Anne Stammage,

Joan Disborrow,

Margaret Gray,

George Eade.

Matthew Hodson,

In 1658, there were imprisoned in the same place,

Joan Disborrow,

*Edward Grant,

John Hall,

John Child, of Felstead, and Anne, his wife,

John Chandler,

Anne Stammage, of Colchester, who was also stoned in the street of Dedham,

* In Crisp's "Testimony" concerning Edward Grant ("Works" p. 358), we learn that when about seventy, he was so violently beaten by the troopers who came to disturb the meeting, that he died a month after, 6th Feb. (1670).

William Simpson, of Billericay, and
Robert Debnam.

1658. 21st Mar. John Daveage, of Burnham, taken to
Chelmsford, and kept several weeks, for "speaking to a priest
in the steeplehouse."

John Eve, of Much Easton, and Anne Child, of Felstead,
were committed to prison at Thaxted.

George Rofe (see No. 102) was kept five weeks in confinement at Saffron Walden, by an order from John Reynolds,
and Samuel Leader, justices.

1658. Aug. John Addams, of Hadstock, was sent to Colchester Castle, at the suit of Thomas Wallis, vicar. He
remained there six months, and was then removed to the
Fleet, where he was kept five months, and then had his goods
distrained.

Widow Ball, and her son William, of Hor[ke]sley, imprisoned at Colchester Castle, at the suit of John Wright, vicar of
Horsley. William Ball was kept some months, although
occupying no land.

Andrew Smith, of Stebbing, was subpæned to appear before
the Barons of Exchequer. He was committed to Colchester
Castle, where he remained seven months, was thence removed to the Common Bench prison at Westminster, and
finally committed to the Fleet, where he remained four
months, and was afterwards distrained upon, to the value of
£20.

John Pollard, of Steeple Grange, was imprisoned at the
Upper Bench prison for ten months, at the suit of Benjamin
Maddock.

John and Joseph Pollard were imprisoned at the Fleet, at
the suit of Josias Armiger.

1658. Henry Smith, of Saling,
Edward Morrell, of Thaxted, and
James Potter, of Mark's Tey,

were sent to Colchester Castle for non-payment of tithes.

1659. Thomas Eltom, and John Eve sent to Colchester Castle.

In March, 1660, Henry Fell, for addressing the people in the churchyard at Saffron Walden, was roughly handled with stones and clods of earth, until blood was shed. Mary Born, and Zachary Child were similarly treated at Felstead.

Anne Langley, and her companion, Anne Stammage, were committed to prison in Colchester, by John Radhams, Mayor in 1659, for entering St. Peter's Church. She probably attempted a protest, as she seems to have been quite undaunted in advancing her principles. She it was who held the dying head of Parnel.

The following were imprisoned for tithes in Colchester Castle :—

> John Crosier of Felstead,
> Moses Davey, of Felstead,
> Robert Abbot, Colne Engaine,
> Thomas Mumford, and Anthony Page, who were kept four years,
> Francis Marriage,* Stebbing,
> John Choppen [Chopping], Stebbing.

Copy of a Pass, dated Colchester, 18th of June, 1660, commanding all constables to convey Thomas Everet, described as a wandering rogue, and disturber of the peace, to Bury St. Edmunds, where he confesses he was born, and last settled, and there to set him on work, or otherwise provide for him. He is assigned to be at Bury St. Edmonds within four days, at his peril ; subscribed, Thomas Peeke, Mayor.

1660. 13th Dec. The Friends hereunder named were taken out of the meeting at Hadstock by troopers, and driven to Saffron Walden, imprisoned in one room, and forwarded to Dunmow, thence to Chelmsford, whence all but two were committed to Colchester Castle.

| John Harvey, | George Corte, |
| John Webb, | Samuel Peachey, |

---

* Kept for twelve months from 1657.

Cottage at Saling, Essex, formerly part of Meeting House, 1675.

Sam. Read,	Jacob Baker,
Walter Crane,	John Simon,
John Churchman,	George Churchman,
Robert Churchman,	John Claiden,
John Day,	Thomas Amye,
Edm. Clark,	Tho. Day,
Jo. Stinton,	John Ellis,
Michell Pettit.	

They were discharged at the Chelmsford Assizes, begun the 18th of March, 1661.

1660. 20th Dec. The following Friends were committed to the Moot Hall, at Colchester, in the custody of James Bloomfield, keeper of the same, for refusing the oath of allegiance :—

John Ingall,	Zachary Welsh,
Joseph Burnish,	Jo. Disbrough,
Edward Grant, the younger,	Thomas Mosse,
Nicholas Prigge,	Michael Thorne,
Edwin Harrison,	John Cooch,
Richard Quick,	Thos. Shortland,
Thomas Bailes,	Nath. Plumstead,
John Complin,	Jo. Bishop,
George Weatherly,	William Quick,
John Patridge,	Zachary Catchpool,
John Havens,	Thomas Burgis.

1660. 24th Dec. John Furly, of Colchester, for refusing the oath of allegiance, was committed to prison at the Moot Hall. The following month, at the Sessions, he was again offered the oath, and again committed, without bail or manieprise. A note is added by Furly himself, showing that this proceeding was illegal, inasmuch as no one magistrate could legally tender an oath, and stating that his imprisonment lasted twelve weeks.

1661. 8th & 21st Jan. William Palmer, William Marlow, John Vanderwall, and Edward Boyce were committed at

Harwich, by Arthur Hawk, Mayor, for refusing the oaths of allegiance and supremacy. They were kept three months.

1661. 13th Jan. Daniel Deacon, of Colchester, also imprisoned.

1661. 20th Jan. William Williams, Thomas Brewer, and Peter Peachy were imprisoned in Colchester Castle for not taking the oath of allegiance.

1661. 20th Jan. John Rolf, of Colchester, committed at Tollesbury, to the Castle, for the same offence.

1661. 20th Jan. The following men were taken from a meeting a Edwin Morrell's house at Thaxted, and, refusing to swear, they were committed to prison for three months :—

> Joseph Smith,
> William Bridge,
> John Harding,
> *Griffen Perry,
> George French,
> John Knowls,
> Thom. Ellis,
> Tho. Sewell,
> William Sewell,
> William Adcock,
> John Turner,
> Joseph Clark.

1661. 27th Jan. The following were apprehended at the same place, a week later, and committed for eleven weeks, viz., Edwin Morrell, John Potter, Griffen Perry, Thomas Eve, Thomas Eltom, John Clark, and Richard Sewell.

1661. 27th Jan. John Salmon, William Hudson, Thomas Lea, John Craven, and John Davedge were taken by soldiers from a meeting at Steeple, in Dengie-hundred, and carried

---

* Griffen Perry lived at Hanningfield, and was trustee of the first meeting-house at Chelmsford, about 1695.

to Southminster, where, refusing the oath, they were committed to Colchester Castle.

DISTRAINTS.

"The 3rd of the 8th mo. [Oct.], 1657. Taken from Georg Weatherlie, for not sending for armes, by Sigismund Baker, Marck Stephen, John Dehorne, serjeants, and henery bell, connstable, one red rugg, and one warming pan, that came to ye sum of twentie and five shillings.

"Then from Georg Weatherley were taken, for ye same thing, upon ye 9th of ye 9th mo. [Nov.], 1667, by ye same three serjeants, as followeth :—One riding cloth coat, vallewed at 8s., one stuffe coate, 3s., and a brass mortar and pessel at 3s., and one whight ockonne* sugar box at 3s., which for both times, the goods in all taken, doe amonnt unto ye sum of 2lb. 0s. 6d.

"At same time, taken by the said officers, from Thomas Cole, for £3 fine, a horse worth eight pounds."

1667. 25th of Oct. Distrained of John Furly, then Junior, for a fine of ten pounds, for not sending in arms, 35 bars of iron, and a pair of large new fire racks, value £14.

From Solomon Freemantell, fine cloth, and a clock worth 50s.

1671. 4th of July. From John Furly, junior, three quarters of a hundred, and thirteen pounds weight of brass kettles.

1670. On the 29th of May, constables and officers, with a warrant signed by Henry Lamb mayor, and John Shaw recorder, came to break up a meeting at Colchester ; the Friends, however, remained until the usual time. On the 26th of June, the Mayor and other officers came again for the same purpose, and ordered out the men one by one, taking their names, and laying the fine of some that were poor upon those more able. On the 2nd of July, the meeting-house doors were locked, and on their being broken open,

---

* Oaken.

the Mayor came on the 11th, and said he seized the house for
the King. The following day, he employed a carpenter and
a mason to plank and brick up the doors and windows, so
that the meeting was then held in the street. The 27th of
the same month, after meeting outside, an entrance was
endeavoured by the Friends a second time into the house,
and before sunset the planks and brickwork had been removed ; but the same night, Matthew Everett, John
Hallaway, and Mary Bray were arrested, and committed to
prison for opening the said house. They were kept there
three weeks. On the Saturday following, the doors were
once more blocked, and so remained until the 4th of Jan.
1671, when the obstacles having been in the morning removed, a quiet meeting was held in the afternoon, and
another five days afterwards. The following day, however,
the meeting-house was again bricked up by the order of
William Moor, [the next] mayor, and so it continued until
the 27th of March, 1671, when the house being hired by a
tenant, the meetings were again resumed, and continued
peaceable.

The following were distrained upon for the act against
meetings (Conventicle Act) :—

Solomon Freemantel, eight bay lists.

Thomas Shortland, a bar of iron worth 7s.

John Bryant, eight bay lists.

Jeptha Solly, yarn.

These lived in the parish of St. James.

"Thomas Everit for a 5s. fine, had taken from him five
pairs of shoes, worth about 9s. Matthew Everit, of St. Nicholas
parish, had taken from him two pieces of an iron stove, which
rendered the other part of the stove of no use. The stove
cost about £4.

"John Furly, minimus, fined 5s., had three leather-back
stools taken from him, worth 14s., by two constables, a warden,
and overseer. These were afterward returned again by another hand. Robert Morffe, fined 55s., [it] being for himself

and ten more, had taken from him two simpatanies, and four yards of broad cloath, worth £5 4s. ; John Havens, fined 35s., had taken from him four hides, worth 48s."

James Read, of St. Peters parish, fined 5s., had taken from him a pair of fire racks.

Thomas Cole, of Lexden, for himself and his son, fined 10s. ; had taken from him a musket, and his son's coat, and a spit.

Thomas Brown, weaver, of St. Giles parish, fined 5s., had taken from him two pewter dishes, and a brass skillet.

"Avery Sanders, fined 5s., had taken from him a mortell and pestell, a pewter platter, and pewter candlestick worth 6s.

Isaac Potter, of Buttolphs parish, had taken from him, by the same officers, a round table.

Tho. Chittam, fined 5s., had taken a brass kettle, and skillet, and a joynt stool, valued at 6s.

Jno. Bishop, fined 5s., had taken from him two iron potts.

Wm. Hadly, of St. Martins parish, fined 5s., had taken from him by Jno. English, constable, and some other officers, the Mayor, Henry Lamb, being psent, a blanket, a chaire, a pillow, and pillow-beer, and pewter platter, valued at 14s.

Richard Allen, of ye Hith, fined, distrained two timber trees.

Sarah Seabrook, of Much Clacton, was sent to Chelmsford Gaol upon a *capias capiendo* at the suit of Thomas Osborn, churchwarden of Much Clacton, for not paying church rate.

Steven Crisp, senior, fined 5s., had taken from him two blankets valued at 10s."

APPENDIX A.

THE WILL OF STEVEN CRISP.°

MEMORANDUM. That upon this three and twenty day of May, in the fourth year of the reignes of William and Mary, King and Queen of England, *anno domi* 1692, I Steven Crisp of Colchester in the county of Essex, weaver, being thorow the mercy of God in good health and of sound disposing mind and memory, calling to mind the frailty of this mortal life, do for the setling my estate which God hath pleased to give me, make and ordaine this my last will and testament in manner and forme following, hereby revoking and making void all former and other wills by me made. *Imprimis* : I give and bequeath to my friends Ruth Crouch,† and Mary Wats, of London, twenty pounds for them to dispose of as they shall see meet. Item : I doe give and bequeath to my friends Anna Talcot, and Elizabeth Furly of Colchester, twenty pounds for them to dispose of as they shall see meet. *Item* : I doe give and bequeath to my three cozens John Crisp, Saml. Crisp, and Thomas Crisp, all of Colchester, five pounds apeece over and above what they owe me at the time of my death, and to Steven Crisp, the son of Samuel Crisp, I give ten pounds to be employed for the putting him out as an apprentice, or if he will not be put out, then to remain in the hand of my Exors, to be pd him at the age of one and twenty yeares, and to the rest of the children of the said Samuel I give twenty shillings apeece. *Item* : I doe give unto Matth. Waller, and Steven Waller, sons of Richard Waller, five and twenty pound apeece, to be paid them by their father when they attaine their respective ages of one and twenty yeares, in discharge of a bond I have of his to pay 50 pounds to my appointment at six months after my decease, and my [will] is that during the said children's minority, Richard Waller shall in every year between Midsummer and Michs. lay out ten shillings apeece in fireing for each of the inhabitants that now are, or hereafter shall be, dwellers in the foure little homes wch I built in Nicholas psh, in Colchester, in all 40 shillings a year for the interest of the fifty pounds, till he pays it as aforesaid.

° Preserved among the archives of the Archdeaconry of Colchester at Somerset House.

† Wife of William Crouch, in whose house he died.

Item : I doe give to Gertrude Losevelt, daughter of Cornelius Losevelt, my bed as it stands, and all the rest of my furniture of my parlour (except my clock and green couch), to be kept for her by some of my Exors until she be sixteen years of age, and then to be delivered to her. *Item* : I doe give my clock to my cozen Richard Waller, and my green couch to Sibilla Adson. My wearing cloths, both linen and woolen, I give to be divided equally among my extors. *Item* : I give to Sarah Hale, the wife of John Hale, the sum of five pounds. *Item* : I doe give to Wm. Hadly, John Hadly, Jas. Catchpoole, John Quennell, and James Babbs, forty shillings apeece. *Item* : I give to the poor of Buttolphs psh in Colchester, three pounds. *Item* : I give to all the children of my brother in law, John Hix, 40 shillings apeece, to be paid them at their respective ages of one and twenty. *Item* : I doe give and bequeath unto [Wm.] Crouch, and his wife, and to Michael Lovell and his wife, three pounds apeece, to Jaswell Crouch, John Crouch, and Ruth Crouch, jr.,° to each of them a guinea. *Item* : My watch I give to my loving friend Sibilla Adson, and my express will is that my Extors shall truly and faithfully pay and satisfy every pson that hath credit in my bookes, for any sum or sumes of money which I have been entrusted with. *Item* : I doe give to my cozen Samuel Crisp of London, and to his wife, each of them a guinea, and I do nominate, constitute, and appoint my loving cozens, Sol. Freemantel, John Furly, and Richard Waller, all of Colchester, to be my exors of this my last will and testament, and doe give them five pound apeece. And my will is that when they have paid and discharged all my debts, trusts, and legacies, or deducted out of my estate so much as will satisfy the same, so that the overplus may appear, that then my extors shall open their accts to my loving friends Willm Colt, Thos Bayles, Dan. Vanderwall, and Henry Pomfrett, and shall bestow and employ the said overplus to such use and uses as they the survivor and survivors of them, shall from time to time direct and appoint, keeping a faire account thereof so long as any of it remains. In witness unto this my will, written all with my owne hand, I have set my hand and seal the day and year above written.

In the presence of Rich. Day, Will. Corbott, Ann Davy.

Steuen Crisp

° Children of William Crouch.

APPENDIX B.

—

A bundle, consisting of twenty-nine papers by Steven Crisp, is deposited in Box A of the MSS. preserved at Devonshire House. They are all endorsed in Benjamin Furly's writing, as having been looked over and read, most of them on the 31st of January, 1693, and "judged not needful to be printed."

They are as follows :—

1. A Christian Reprehension, &c., on a conceited pamphlet ; by G.W. and S.C., 1690.
2. The Touchstone Touched, in answer to H.C.H., of Harlingen, in Freesland.
3. A Letter to Dr. Andreas, president at Embden.
4. An Epistle to Friends : " Dear Lambs, &c."
5. A Cry against Persecution begun and carryed on by ye rulers and presidents in Freesland.
6. A Paper concerning Marriage.
7. An Answer to Jacob Picters.
8. A True Relation of a grievous Lye, &c. [Dutch, printed in *Collectio*, p. 446.]
9. An English Translation of the same.
10. To Marten Arents, 16th August, 1670.
11. S.C. to Friends about John Harwood.
12. My Answer to Ab. Jansen, of Goch, Germany, a Baptist.
13. To ye Magistrates of Embden, September, 1675. In print in Dutch. Yˢ is ye original ?
14. A Letter to a Magistrate, P.P.
15. Letter from Crisp and his fellow prisoner, Samuel Hawkins, from the County Gaol in Ipswich, to the Magistrates, 27th of May, 1670.
16. To William Woolley, of Harwich.
17. To Parson Long.

18. To Samuel Hassell, of Sudbury, dated Ipswich, 3rd of April, 1670. From one who is a friend to good magistrates, and true ministers, and a witness against the contrary.
19. To ye Mayor of Cambridge.
20. To ye Justices of ye Peace for ye County of Durham.*
21. S.C.'s Letter to ye Lieutenancy in Durham.
22. To Friend R.T. [endorsed by Furly, " I know not who it is."]
23. To Justice Eldred, Harwich, 25th September, 1662.
24. To John Eldred, Justice, near Colchester.
25. To Richard Howlett, a Priest.
26. To ye King.
27. An Epistle to a private person.
28. A Letter to Antoinette Bourignon, Amsterdam, 18th of March, 1669, respecting a book by her, called *An Excellent Letter, &c.*
29. A letter to a Friend, Hermann Witts.
30. Truth triumphing over Falsehood, in answer to a book on Religious Worship, by Alexander Ross, 1670.

In Box C there is also :

An information unto Charles II., King of England, signed by Steven Crisp, Robert Letchworth, Nicholas Frost, John Deane, dated Cambridge, 16th of July, 1660.

This Address was delivered by Margaret Fell to the King. (See Besse's Sufferings Ed. 1753, vol. 1, p. 88.)

---

* See Introduction, pp. xxii., xxiii., xxiv.

INDEX.

	PAGE
Abbey Rippon - - -	7
Abbis, Rinck - - -	35
Abbot, Robert - - -	70
Aberdeen - 12, 22, 51, 52, 55	
Abrahams, Galenus - xlii. 64	
Act of Uniformity - -	7
Addams, John - - -	69
Adcock, William- - -	72
Addison (or Adson), Sibilla-	77
Alexandria - - - -	4
Algiers - - - xxxvi.	
Alkmaer - - - xxxiii. 18	
Allen, Richard - - -	75
Allerthorpe, Yorks - -	36
Alresford - - - xxxii.	
Altenburgh- - - -	38
Altmore - - - -	62
Alton - - - - xxxii.	
America - 13, 31, 51, 52, 55	
Ames, William - - xxxix. 17	
Amsterdam x. xxvii. xxviii. xxix.	
xxxiii. xxxiv. xxxv. xxxvi.	
xxxix. xli. xlii. xliii. l. li. 1,	
14, 15, 16, 17, 18, 24, 25, 27,	
34, 35, 58, 59,60, 66, 79.	
New Bridge St. 35, Prince	
Straat 37, Prince's Island 35,	
Vish Steege xli.	
Amye, Thomas - - -	71
Anderslow - - -	50
Andover - - - xxxii. 8	
Andreas, Christian - -	33
———— Cornelis - -	53
———— Dr. - -	78
Appleby Gaol - - -	50
Arents, Jacob - 24, 33	
———— Martin - - -	78
———— Peter - - -	34
———— Walter - - -	30
Armiger, Josias - - -	69
Arnheim - - - -	38
Arksey - - - 14, 42	
Armagh - - - -	55
Arminius - - - -	30
Arnside - - - -	52
Arundel - - - -	43
Ashfield, Richard - - xxx.	
Aspatria - - - -	54
Audland, John - - -	48
Austria - - - -	46
Babbs, James - - -	77
Bacharach - - - -	38
Baker, Jacob - - -	71
———— Sigismund - -	73
Bakker, John de - - -	30
Balc - - - -	47
Ball, Widow - - -	69
—— William - - -	69
Baptists - - - xxvii.	
Barbadoes - xliii. 13, 30, 31, 40,	
41, 48, 56, 58, 60.	
Barclay, Colonel David - 22	
———— Robert ix. x. xli. xlii.	
xlvii. 1, 2, 3, 12, 22, 25, 26, 28.	
Barnardiston, Giles 9, 43, 59, 60, 62	
Barrington, Richard - -	39
Barrow, Robert - xlvi. 51	
Barwick, Dr. John - - xxiv.	
Bath - - - xxx. 4	
Batten - - - - xxxi.	
Bayles, Thomas xviii. 34, 48, 49,	
59, 60, 71, 77.	
Baysmaking - - xv. xvi.	
Beacon, Nicholas - -	68
Beale, Thomas - - -	43
Beets, Jacob - - -	30
Bedfordshire - - -	59
Beeford - - - -	25
Bell, Henry - - -	73
Bellarbutt - - -	54
Bellasis, Captain - - xxii.	
Bellers, Francis - - -	40
———— John - - -	41
Bennet, Elizabeth - -	11
Berlin - - - -	15
Bermuda - - - -	30
Bethick - - - - xxxi.	
Beveridge, Rev. John - -	50
Beverley - - - - 26, 2	
Bingen - - - -	38
Bird, Richard - - -	58
Bisbrown, Margaret - -	52
Bishop, John - - 71, 75	

	PAGE
Blackley, Ann - - -	3, 4
———— James - - -	3
Black Spread Eagle - -	18
Blaykling, John - -	- 2, 34
Blewberry - - -	- xxx.
Bloomfield, James -	- 71
Bodmin - - -	- xxxi.
Boehme, Jacob - -	- 38
Bohemia, Queen of -	xi. 20
Bolsward - - -	- 33
Bonn - - - -	- 38
Boome, Mary Ann -	- 38
Boppart - - -	- 38
Born, Mary - - -	- 70
Boston - - -	56, 57
Boucher, Mr. - -	- 37
Bourignon, Antoinette-	- 79
Bowdinune, Bowdin -	- 30
Boxted - - -	- 57
Boyce, Edward -	xxv. 37, 71
Brabrooke, Thomas -	- 49
Bradey, Mary - -	- 68
Bradford, Mrs. E. -	- 14
Braintree - - -	- 6
Bray - - -	- xxxi.
—— Mary - -	18, 74
Bremen - - -	xxxii.
Breslau - -	- 15, 16, 17
Brewer, Thomas - -	- 72
Bridport - - -	- xxxi.
Bridge, William - -	- 72
Bridgetown - -	- 31
Brill, The - - -	- 28
Bristol - xxx. xxxiv.	48, 56
Brookes, William -	- 40
Brown, Alderman Richard -	4
—— Sir Richard -	- 60
—— Ruth - -	- 9
—— Thomas -	31 75
Bryan, Sir Francis -	- xlvi.
Bryan's Wood -	xlvi. 29
Bryant, John - -	- 74
Buchanan - -	- 39
Bundack, Jonathan -	- 68
Bunhill Fields -	xlviii.
Burgess, Samuel -	- xxx.
———— Thomas	- 71
Burnham - -	67, 69
Burnish, Joseph -	- 71
Burnyeat, John - 54. 55, 56, 57, 58
Burrough, Edward	- xxvii. 3, 8
Bury St. Edmunds -	- 70
Byllinge, Edward -	- 25
Calne - - -	- xxx.

	PAGE
Cambridge xxi. xxii. 3, 4, 5, 16, 44, 79.	
Cameronians - -	- 52
Campagne, Joseph -	- 37
Cannon, John - -	- 29
Carlisle - -	- 5, 54
Carlow - - -	- 55
Carolina - -	- 31
Carrickfergus - -	- 55
Carter, Clement -	- 11
Carthaginians - -	- 52
Cascetter, Manasseh -	- liv.
Castle Hedingham -	- 67
Catchpool, James -	- 77
———— Zachary -	- 71
Cater, Ezekiel - -	- 5, 71
—— Samuel xxx. xxxiii. 5, 6
Caton, William xi. xxvii. xxxvii. xxxviii. xxxix. 27, 33, 59.
—— Annekin xxxvi, xxxvii. xxxviii. xxxix. xli. xliii. 27, 59, 60.
Cavan, County - -	- 54
Chandler, John - -	- 68
Charles I. - - -	- xlvii.
Charles II., xxi. xxiii. 3, 22, 52, 79
Charles IX.- - -	53
—— Louis, Elector Palatine - xxix. 21, 22, 28.
—— Ludovic, Emperor -	31
Cheevers, Sarah - - -	4
Chelmsford 44, 67, 69, 70, 71, 72, 75.
Child, Anne - -	68, 69
—— John - -	xxv. 68
—— Thomas - -	- xix.
—— Zachary - -	xx. 70
Chippenham - -	- xxx.
Chittani, Thomas -	- 75
Chopping, John - -	- 70
———— Stephen -	- xix.
Churchman, George -	- 71
———— John -	- 71
———— Robert -	- 71
Clacton, Great or Much -	67
Claes, Jeske - -	- 35
Claidon, John - -	68, 71
Clare - - -	43, 44
Claridge, Richard -	- x. 9
Clark, Edmund - -	- 71
—— John- - -	- 72
—— Joseph - -	- 72
—— R.- - -	- 14
Clark, Samuel - -	- 9

PAGE

Claus, Jacob - 15, 18, 37, 66
—— Jan xxix. xxxiv. xxxvii.
l., 15, 17, 18, 24, 33, 38, 45.
Cleves - - - - 38
Cleveland - - - - liv.
Cliff, Rev. John - - - 9
Clothall - - - - 29
Coale, Josiah - xii. xxviii. 48
Cock, Giles - - - 62
Coggeshall - - xviii. 6, 47, 59
Coghen, John - - - 59
Colchester x. xiii. xv. xvi. xvii.
xx. xxv. xxxii. xxxiii. xxxiv.,
xxxvi. xlii. xliii. xlvi. li. 7, 8,
30, 37, 42, 44, 47, 48, 49, 57, 70,
72, 79.
    Almshouse Lane xxxvi. xlv.
49 ; Castle xx. xxv. 7, 68, 69,
70, 72, 73 ; Dutch population in
xviii. ; Eastgate xvii. ; East
Stockwell St. xviii. ; East Street
49, 57 ; Mayors of xviii. xxvi.
12, 31, 68 (2), 70 (2), 73, 75 ;
Monthly Meeting of v. xviii.
xxxvi. xliii. lii. ; Moor Lane x.
xiv. xvii. xviii. 49 ; Moot Hall
xvii. xxv. xxvi. 68, 71 ; St.
Bottolph's 49, 75, 77 ; St. Bottolph's Priory xvii. ; St. Bottolph's
Street xvii. ; St. Giles' 75, 48,
49 ; St. Helen's Chapel xviii. ;
St. Helen's Lane 49 ; St. James'
49, 74 ; St. Martin's 75 ; St.
Martin's Lane xviii. xxvi. 49 ;
St. Mary's Lane xvi. ; St.
Nicholas 6, 49, 74, 77 ; St. Peter's
xvii. 70, 74 ; St. Runwald's xliv. ;
Persecution of Friends in xxv. ;
Priory St. xvii. ; John de 50 ;
The Hythe 57.
Colbrooke - - - - xxx.
Cole, Thomas - - 73, 75
Collegianten - xliii. 16, 28
Collumpton - - - xxxi.
Coleman, Thomas - - xxx
Colne Engaine - - - 70
Cologne - - - 28, 38
Colt, William - - - 77
Complin, John - - - 71
Commonwealth - - - 25
Connecticut - - - 57
Conventicle Act - - 9, 44, 74
Cooch, John - - - 71
Cook, Mary - - - 67

PAGE

Cook, Thomas - - - 6
Copenhagen - - - 32
Crbett, William - - - 77
Cork - - - - xxvi. 55
Cornwall - - - xxxi. 48
Corte, George - - - 70
Cotton, John - - 57 note
—— Seaborn - - - 57
Cox, Eliz. - - - - 60
Council of Scotland - - 2, 3
Crabtreebeck - - - 54
Crane, Walter - - - 71
Craven, John - - - 72
Crefeld - - - xxxv. 18
Crisp, Dorothy xvi. xvii. xxxvi.
    xliii. 13, 17, 18, 59
—— Gertrude xlv. See Dericks
—— John - - xlix. 76
—— Elizabeth, sen. - xiii. xiv.
    xvii. 13, 26
——————————— jun. - - xvii.
——————————— of St. Osyth xxxvi.
—— Samuel - xlix. 76, 77
—— Steven, sen. xiii. xiv. 26, 75
——————— - - passim
——————— jun. - xlix. 76
—— Thomas - xlix. 76
Crockernwell - - xxxi.
Cromwell, Oliver- - 7, 34, 42
———————— Henry - - 51
Crook, John - - 59, 62
Crosier, John - - - 70
Cross, Peter - - - 11
Crosse, Edmund - - - 68
Crouch, Jaswell - - - 77
———— John - - - 77
———— Nathaniel - - l.
———— Ruth - - 9, 76
——————— jun. - - 77
Crouch, William 8, 14, 17, 29, 54,
58, 66, 77.
Crow, William - xix. xx.
————— jun. - xix. xx.
Crow's Green - - - xx.
Cumberland - - 54, 55
Cuyper, Mart - - - 30

Dalkeith - - - xxi.
Dantzic, - xxxv. 18, 24, 27, 32
Davage, John - 68, 69, 72
Davey Moses - - - 70
Davies, Richard - - 47
Davy, Ann - - - 77
Dawson, John - - - 52

	PAGE
Day, John	71
—— Richard	77
—— Thomas	71
Deacon, Daniel	72
Deane, John	79
Debnam, Robert	69
Dedham	68
De Horne, John	73
De Labadie, Jean	22, 36
Dengie Hundred	68, 72
Denmark	xxxii.
Derby	36
Dericks, Annekin xxxvi. xxxvii. xxxviii. xxxix. xli. xliii.	
—— Cornelis	xlv.
—— Gertrude xiii. xxxvi. xxxix. xl. xli. xlii. xliii. xliv. 13, 14, 15, 17, 23, 24 & n., 33, 36, 59, 60, 62.	
—— Neisy xxxvi. xxxvii. xliv. 33	
Descartes, Réné	xi. 21
Dewsbury, William	12, 26, 36
Dickenson, Jonathan	52
Diersdorf	16
Disborrow (or Disbrough), Joan 68, 71.	
Donaghadee	55
Doughty, John	5
Dover	46
—— Castle	43
Draton, Thomas	7
Drawell	34 (2)
Dublin	55, 5
—— Marshalsea Prison	57
—— New Garden	57
Duke of Albemarle	9
—— Buckingham	46
Duke Charles of Munsterberg	16
Duke Frederick of Liegnitz	16
—— of Lauderdale	2, 3
Duchess of Lauderdale	22
Duncon, Robert	59, 62
—— his wife	59
Dunmow	xix. 70
Durham xxii. xxiii. xxxiii. 46, 55, 79.	
Dusseldorf	38
Eade, George	68
East India Company	26
East Riding, Yorks	25, 36, 47
Easton, Great or Much	69
Eccleston, John	26

	PAGE
Eccleston, Theodore	26
Edburton	13
Edinburgh	51, 52
Edmundson, William	57
Edwards, Dr. John	6
Earl of Lauderdale	3
Eldred, Justice	xxv. 79
Electress Louise Juliana	20
Electress Sophia of Hanover	20
Elligood, Richard	5
Ellis, John	xxxi. 71
Ellis, Thomas	72
Eltom, Thomas	70, 72
Elways, Gervase	44
Ely, Isle of	5
Embden x. xxxii. xxxiv. 18, 24, 53, 64, 65, 78.	
Emperor Constantine	49
Emson, John	xix.
Endeavour, The	24
English, John	75
Ennomessike	53
Episcopius, Simon	80
Eppinghooft, L. H. Von	-xxxii.
Essex	li., 6, 7, 27, 40, 44
—— Friends in xviii. xix. xx. 67	
Evans, John	4
—— Katherine	xxx. 4
Eve, John	69, 70
—— Thomas	72
Evener, William	xix.
Everett, Matthew	74
—— Thomas	70, 74
Exeter	xxxi.
Falmouth	xxxi.
Feedham, Edward	xvii. 60, 61
Fell, Henry	70
—— Judge	41
—— Leonard	47
—— Margaret xxii. xliv. l. 41, 70	
Felsted xviii. xx. xxv. 6, 67, 69, 70	
Fenstanton	5
Field, John	xlix.
Fifth Monarchy men	27
Fisher, Samuel	x. 8, 60
Fishlake	14
Fiskerton	47
Fogoe, Priest	54
Forster, Joseph	xx.
Fox, George xiv. xviii. xxii. xxvii. xxxiv. xli. xlii. xlvi. xlvii. 1, 2, 3, 8, 12, 17, 18, 43, 45, 47, 50, 54, 55, 56, 58, 59.	

PAGE

Fox, George, the younger xiv. 19, 44.

—— Justice - - - 45

Foxe, John - - - 37

Fletcher, Lancelot - - 54

Florida, Gulf of - - - 52

Flushing - - - 32

Frederic, John - - - 9

Frederickstadt - - xxxii. 18

Freeman, B. - - - 31

Freemantel, Solomon 11, 18, 26, 49, 59, 74, 77

—— Sarah - 18, 26

French, George - - - 72

Friesland xxviii. xxxiii. xxxv. 1, 18, 27, 28, 35, 64, 78.

Frost, Nicholas - - - 79

Fuce, Joseph - - 43, 60

Fuller, William - - - 10

Furly, Abigail - - - xliv.

—— Ann - xliv. 59, 62

—— Benjamin xl. xli. 1, 11, 12, 18, 22, 29, 43, 49, 59, 78.

—— Elizabeth - - - 76

—— John xvii. xli. xliv. l., 33, 34, 48, 49, 59, 60, 66, 71, 73, 74, 77.

Furnerius, Isaac - - - 30

Gainer, Mary - - - 4

Galway - - - - 56

George I. - - - - 20

—— II. - - - - liii.

General Meeting of Amsterdam 39

Germany xi. xxvii. xxix. xxxviii. xxxix. xli. xlii. 12, 16, 17, 30, 38, 43, 62, 78.

Gestingthorpe - - - 67

Gibson, William - - - 45

Glasgow - - - - 51

Glastonbury - - - xxx.

Goch - - - - 78

Gordon, Catherine - - 22

—— Sir Robert - - 22

Gould, Daniel - - - 56

Gouldney, Henry - - xlvi.

Grand Pensionary - - 1, 20

Grant, Edward - - - 68

—— the younger - 71

Gray, Margaret - - - 68

Greece - - - - 13

Green, Elizabeth - - - 49

Gregory, Stoke St. - - xxxi.

Gregorian Calendar - - lii.

PAGE

Gressingham, Edward - - 19

Griesheim - - - xxix. 38

Groningen - - - x. xxix.

Groome, Samuel - - - 53

Guildford - - xii. xxxv. 48

Gustavus Adolphus - - 34

Gwin, Mayor of Smithwick - 24

Haarlem, xxxiii. xlii. 18, 27, 29, 59, 60.

Haddock - - - - 14

Hadley, William - - - 75

Hadstock - - 67, 68, 69, 70

Hague, The - x. 12, 20, 32

Hall, John - - - - 68

Hallaway, John - - 57, 74

Hale, John - - - - 77

—— Sarah - . - - 77

Halliday, James - - - 51

Halls, Henry - - - 47

—— Elizabeth - - - 47

Halstead - - - - 6, 67

Ham - - - - - xviii.

Hamburg xxxii. xxxv. 13, 15, 18, 27, 52, 58.

Hampshire - - - xxx. 8

Hampton - - - - 56

Happenini, Jedaia - 15, 16

Harding, John - - - 72

Harlackenden, William - 6

Harlingen - - - 27, 78

Harmun, Matthias - - 29

Harper, D. - - - - 42

—— Jane - - - 42

Harrison, Edwin - - - 71

—— J. - - - 42

Hart, Thomas - - - 31

Hartford, Conn. - - - 57

Hartigfelt - - - - 59

Harward, W. - - - 53

Harwich x. xxv. xxxvi. xlii. 14, 19, 71, 78, 79.

Harwood, John - - 43, 78

Harvey, John - - - 70

Hasbert, Dr. - - xxxiv. 18

Hassell, Samuel - - - 79

Hatfield - - - - 14

Havens, John - - 71, 74

—— Mary - - - 59

—— William - - - 59

Hawk, Arthur - - - 71

Hawkins, John - - - 31

—— Samuel - - - 78

Hayes, Mr. - - - - 40

PAGE

Headington - - - xxx.
Heidelberg - xxix. xlii. 20, 38
Helstone - - - - xxxi.
Hendricks, Elizabeth xlii. 13, 15,
16, 17, 23, 36.
———— Peter xxxii. xlii. 14,
15, 18, 24, 30, 33, 45, 58, 59,
62, 63.
Herferd, or Herwerden 19, 21, 23,
36.
Hertford - - - - 59
Hertfordshire - - 25, 29
Heus, Peter - - - 15
Hide, Edmund - - - xxx.
Higgins, John - - 58, 62
Highclere, Hants - - 26
Hillier, Mr. - - - 40
Hills, Judge - - - 7
—— Thomas - - xxx.
Hind, a tanner - - - 5
Hitchcock, William - - xxx.
Hix (or Hicks), John - xlvi. 77
Hodson, Matthew - - 68
Holderness - - - 25, 47
Holland x. xi. xii. xxvii. xxviii.
xxix. xxxii. xxxiii. xxxiv. xxxv.
xxxvi. xxxviii. xxxix. xl. xli.
xlii. xliii. xlix. 1, 11, 12, 18, 21,
30, 32, 35, 42, 44, 45, 48, 58, 59,
60, 64, 66.
Holinton - - - - xxx.
Holm - - - - 51
Holstein - xxxii. xxxv. 1, 28
Hookes, Ellis - - - 8
Horne, Richard - - - 10
Hornes, Countess - - 22
Horkesley - - - - 69
Horsleydown - - xxvii.
Howgill, Francis xxvii. 8, 50
Howlett, Richard - - 79
Hubbersty, Stephen - - 68
Hubberthorn, Richard - - 3, 55
Huberts, Wiardi - - - 53
Hudson, William - - 72
Hull - - - 29, 47
Humber - - - liv.
Hungary - - - 16, 46
Huntingdonshire - 5, 7, 51
Hurst - - - - 19
Hutchinson, Dorothy - 25, 36
———— Thomas - 26, 29
Inglishcombe - - - 4
Indians - - - - 52
Ingall, John - - - 71

PAGE

Inquisition - - - - 71
Ipswich xxvi. xxxii. liv. 31, 43, 59,
78, 79.
Ireland - 4, 52, 53, 55, 56, 57
Ismaed, Arthur - - - xxx.
Isaac, John - - - 67
Italy - - - - - 13

Jacobites - - - xlviii.
Jacobs, J. - - - xxxii. 13
———— Isaac - - 13, 33, 64
Jaffray, Andrew - - - 52
James I. - - xi. 20, 22
———— II. - - xlvi. 36
Jamaica - - - 13, 18, 43
Jansen, Ab. - - - 78
———— Hester - - - 53
———— Mary - - - 34
Jenner Thomas - - - 9
Jersey, East - - . 25
———— West - - 25
Jesper, John - - - xix.
John, Martin - - - 38
Johnson, Katherine - - 58
Julian Calendar - - - lii.

Keith, George xli. xlii. 12, 16, 42
———— his wife xlii. 23
Kember, Johannes - - 2
Kendal - - - - 62
Kendall, John - - ix. xl.
Kent - - - - 36
Kilkenny - - - - 55
King of Bohemia - - 20
———— Poland - - 21
Kingsbridge - - - xxxi.
King's Ripton - - - 51
Kingston - - 27, 41, 43
Kingswell - - 51, 52
Kleermaker, Edward de - 26
Knoll, Jan Kornelis - - 62
Knowls, John - - - 72
Kynance - - - - xxxi.

Lamb, Henry - - 73, 75
Lambert, Colonel - - 50
Lambourne - - - xxx.
Lancashire - - xxi. 3, 50
Lancaster - xlvi. 25, 26, 62
Lancaster, James - - 56
Land's End - - xxx. xxxi.
Landtsmeer - - - 30
Lane, John - - - xix.
Langley, Ann - - 8, 68, 70

PAGE

Langley, Peter - - - 48
Latemus, Canon James - 30
Laubgrund - - - - 38
Launceston - - - xxxi. 48
Lawrence, John - - - 11
Lawrie, Gawen - - 24, 25
———— George - - 11, 29 (2)
Lawson, Thomas - - - x.
———— Wilfrey - - 5
Lea, Thomas - - - 72
Lead, Mrs. Jane - - - 35
Leader, Samuel - - - 69
Leavens, John - - - 47
Leclerc, Jean - - - 12
Lee, Dr. Francis - - - 36
Leeuwarden - xxxiii. 33, 64
Leghorn - - - - 4
Lemon, John - - - 39
———— Margaret - - 39
———— Nicholas - - - 39
———— Sarah - - - 39
———— Thomas - - - 39
Lenz - - - - - 38
Letchworth, Robert - - 79
Levitt, Joseph - - - xix.
Lexden - - - xl. 75
Leyden - 30, 58, 59, 60, 62
Limborch, Philip van - 12
Lincoln - - - liv. 27, 47
Lincolnshire - xxi. liv. 46, 47
Linde, Thomas - - - 11
Littleport - - - - 5
Lizard, the - - xxxi.
Locke, John - - xi. 12
Lodge, John - - 24, 62
———— Robert - - 47, 54, 55
London, xviii. xxviii. xxx. xxxii.
xxxv. xlvi. xlvii. 1, 7, 8, 14,
16, 18, 19, 25, 40, 41, 42, 44, 56,
58, 62.
  All Hallows, Lombard Street
13; Bishopsgate 58; Broad Street
Ward 9; Bull & Mouth, Aldgate
4 ; Cheapside 43, 54 ; Covent
Garden 40 ; Crown Court xlviii.
9, 40; Devonshire House xxii.
xxxv. xlviii. l. 57, 58, 65, 78 ;
Devonshire Square 51 ; Finch
Lane 9 ; Fleet Prison 69 ; Grace-
church Street xlviii. l. 9, 54, 66 ;
Grafton Street 37 ; Houndsditch
44 ; Lambeth House 19 ; Mayor
of 9 ; Newgate 4, 36, 47, 57 ;
Old Bailey 18 ; Peel Meeting 9 ;

PAGE

Plaistow Meeting 17 ; Poultry
Compter 9 ; St. Bennets 9 ; St.
Bennet Fink 9 ; Tower 43 ;
Turner's Hall 13 ; Vere Street
40 ; Westminster 69 ; West-
minster Gate House 9 ; White-
hall 8 ; White Hart Court xlvi. 9 ;
White Lion, Southwark 43.
Londonderry - - - 54
Long, Parson - - - 78
Longford - - - - xxx.
Long Island - - - 56
Longworth, Roger - - 38
Lorton - - - - 54
Losevelt, Adrain van xxxix. xl.
xli. 59.
———— Cornelis xliv. xlv. xlix.
77.
———— Gertrude, jun. xlix. 77
Lower, Humphrey - - xxxi.
Loweswater - - - 54
Lucas, Nicholas - - - 25
Luther, Martin - - 16, 17
Lutherans - - 2, 15, 16, 17
Luton - - - - 59
Lynn - - - - liv. 43

Macronain, Johannem - - 53
Maddock, Benjamin - - 69
Maitland - - - - 39
Malam, Bartholomew - - xxx.
Maldonat, Jean - - 37 & n
Malta - - - - - 4
Mansfield, Edward - - xix.
———— John - - xx.
Marier - - - - 53
Marriage, Francis xix. xxv. 70
Marks Tey - - - 69
Marlborough - - - xxx.
Marlow, William - xxxvi. 71
———— Grace - xxxvi.
Martin, William - xxv. 37
Maryland, 29, 30, 31, 36, 48, 53, 56
Marywood, Widow - - 40
Mason, Martin - - - 13
Massy, J. - - - - 42
Methsias, Archduke - - 53
Meath - - - - 54
Meeting for Sufferings 29, 67
Meers, Sir Thomas - - 40
Melton Gaol - - - 11
Membury - - - - xxxi.
Mendlesham - - - 59
Menno Simons - xxvii. xxix. 27

	PAGE		PAGE
Mennonites - -	16, 27, 28,66	Osborne, Thomas - -	75
Metz - - - -	38	Osgood, John - - -	24
Milford Haven - - -	56	—— Thomas - - -	8
Moate - - - -	54	Osyth, St. - -	xiv. xxxvi.
Molleson, Gilbert - -	52	Owis (or Howis), Solomon -	39
—— Margaret - -	52	Owstwicke - - -	25, 36, 47
Moore Thomas - - -	8		
Moore, William xxv. xxvi. 46, 74		Page, Anthony - - -	70
Moort - - - -	59	Painter, Mary - - -	39
Morffe, Robert - -	58, 74	Palatinate, the - - -	20
Mors - - - -	38	Palsgrave, the - - -	xxix.
Mortlake - - - . -	26	Palmer, William - - -	71
Morrell, Edward - - -	69	Parke, James 17, 45, 47, 62, 63	
—— Edwin - - -	72	Parker, Alexander -	29, 45
Morris, Lewis - - -	58	Parliament - - -	51, 52
Mosse, Thomas - - -	71	—— House - -	40
Mosyer, John - - -	39	Parnel, James xvii. xxxiii. xxxiv.	
Mott, Councillor - - -	39	4, 5, 6, 7, 8, 70.	
—— William -	xvii. 68	Patridge (or Partridge), John	71
Mount, Thomas - -	- xxxi.	Peachey, John - - . xix. liv.	
Mountmellick - - -	55	—— Peter - - -	72
Mügge, Michael - -	32	—— Samuel - -	70
—— Jacob - -	32	Peeke, Thomas - - -	70
—— his wife - -	32	Pelham, Herbert - -	6
Muggleton, Ludovic - -	48	Penn, William ix. x. xii. xli. xlii.	
Mumford, Robert - -	70	xliii. xlvii. 2, 12, 17, 22, 24, 64.	
Munster - - - -	55	Pennington, I. - - -	43
Mysticism - - - -	36	Pennslyvania xii. xiii. xlvii. 17,	
		18, 42, 52.	
Nayler, James - -	50, 51	Pennyman, John - -	24
Neat, Thomas - -	- xxx.	Pensionary, the - -	1, 2, 12
Newcastle - - -	52	Penton-by-Wayhill - -	8
New England 30, 41, 53, 56, 58		Perrot, John - -	13, 56
New Jersey - - -	31	Perry, Griffen - - -	72
New Style - - -	- liii.	Person (or Pierson), Lambert	33
New York - - -	xiii., 56	Pettit, Michael - - -	71
Nicholas, John - -	- xxiv.	Philadelphia - -	24, 52
Niesen, Gertrude See Dericks.		Philadelphians - -	36
Norfolk - - -	liv., 47	Philadelphia Quakers - -	12
Northampton - -	25, 36	Philley, John - -	43, 46
Northumberland - - -	51	Philpot Lane - - -	40
Norton - - -	- xxii.	Pickering, William - -	5
—— Humphrey -	43, 45	Place, Francis - - -	51
—— Mary - - -	10	Plumstead, Nathaniel - -	71
—— William - - -	10	Plymouth - - xxxi. 24	
Norwich - - -	- liv.	Poland - - - -	32
—— Castle - - -,	3	Pollard, John - - -	69
Nottingham - - -	4, 5	—— Joseph - - -	69
		Polybius - - - -	52
Oaro - - - -	- xxx.	Poludamus, Theodorus -	33
Oldebergh - - -	xxxii. 15	Pomfrett, Henry - -	liv. 77
Oldeslow - - - -	1	Poole - - - -	xxxi.
Opauki, Albertus - -	32	—— Samuel - -	47
Orlingen - - - -	38	—— Christopher - -	47

PAGE

Pool, Simon de - - 32, 66
Pope, the - - - - 13
Portsmouth- - xxx. xxxi. 43
Potter, James - - - 69
—— Isaac - - - 75
—— John - - - 72
Prache, Hilary - 15, 16, 17, 28
Prigge, Nicholas - - - 71
Prince Palatine - - - 38
—— Rupert - - 22, 51
Princes Island - - - 35
Princess Elizabeth xi. xlii. 2, 19,
23, 36.
—— Louise - - - 20
Proclamation of Toleration - 53
Providence - - - - 57
Puritans - - - 6
Pyl, Simon van der - - 32

Quedlinburg - - - x.
Quennell, John - - - 77
Quick, Richard - - - 71
—— William - - - 71

Radhams, John - - - 70
Raoul, Noah - - - 42
Rasleton - - - - 10
Ray, John - - - - 5
Read, James - - - 74
—— Samuel - - - 71
Reading - - - - xxx.
Redruth - - - - xxxi.
Reformation, the - - 17
Regensburg - - - 38
Rendlesham - - - 11
Retford - - - - 5
Reynolds, John - - - 69
Rhine, the - - - - xxxv.
Rhode Island - - - 56
Riggs, Anna - - - 10
—— Elizabeth - - 10
—— Edward - - 9, 11
—— Sarah - - - 9
—— Thomas - - - 9
Ringwood - - - - xxxi.
Ripon - - - - 55
Roberts, Gerard - - - 8
Robinson, Thomas - - 45
Robinson the persecutor - xxxi.
Roelofs, Barent - - - 33
—— Cornelius 33, 34, 59, 64
—— Deborah - - - 13
—— Edward - - - 26
—— Jan li., 13, 18, 24, 45

PAGE

Roelofs, Peter - - - 15
Rofe, George - - 30, 31, 69
Rogers, John - - - xxx.
Rolf, John - - - - 72
Rome - - - xxiii., 13
Ross, Alexander - - - 79
Rotterdam xxvii. xxviii. xxxii.
xxxv. 12, 14, 16, 18, 28, 30, 58,
59, 62.
—— South Blaak - xxviii.
Rous, John xi. xliii. 40, 41, 58
—— Lieut.-Col. - - - 41
—— Margaret - - xi. 41

Saffron Walden - 31, 67, 69, 70
Salem - - - - 57
Saling - - - - xix.
Salisbury - - - - 4
Salmeron, Alfonso - - 37
Salmon, John - - - 72
Salthouse, Thomas - - xxxi.
Samms, John - - - 6, 7
Sanders, Avery - - - 75
Sandford - - - - xxxi.
Sandown - - - - 43
Sandwich - - - - 56
Sawyer, Sir Robert - - 26
Saxlingham - - - - 47
Sayer, Gyles - - - 49
Scotland xi. xxi. xliv. xlvii. 22,
51, 52, 55.
Scott, Sir Walter - - - 42
Schwaner, Mark - - - 38
Schwenksfeld, Caspar - 16, 17
Schwenksfelden - - - 16
Shaftesbury, Lord - - 12
Shaw, Sir John - - - 37
—— John - - - 73
Shortland, Susan - - - 31
—— Thomas - 68, 71, 74
Schinkhausen - - - 38
Silesia - - - - 38
Simmons, Martha - - 68
Simson, William - - - 69
Simon, John - - - 71
Simpson, William - - 69
Sitses, Dowie - - - 33
Skillingham, Samuel - - 68
Seabrook, Sarah - - - 75
Sedbergh - - - - 34
Sewel, Bedfordshire - - 59
—— John - - - 67
—— William xi. xxxiii. l. 5, 8,
26, 27, 59.

	PAGE
Sewell, Richard - - -	73
——— Thomas - - -	72
——— William - - -	72
Seymour, Mr. - - -	40
Slaughterford - - -	xxx.
Smith, Andrew - xxxv.	69
——— H. - - -	60
——— Henry - -	xx. 69
——— John - - xix. xxxii.
——— Joseph - - -	72
——— William - - -	8
——— Steven - -	-xxxii.
Socinians - - -	xlii.
Solly, Jeptha - - -	74
Somersetshire - -	-xxvii.
Sorbière, Samuel - -	21
Southampton - -	-xxxi.
Southminster - -	-67, 72
Spalding - - -	-27, 47
Sparrow, William - -	6
Spinola, Marquis - -	20
Staffordshire - -	25
St. Alban's - - -	43
Stalham, John - -	6, 7
Staines - - -	xxx.
Stammage, Ann - -	-68, 70
Stanway - - -	xxv.
Starling, Sir Samuel - -	57
Start, John - - -	xix.
Stebbing - xix. xx. 6, 41, 69, 70
Steeple - - -	-69, 72
Stephen, Mark - -	73
Stinton, Jo. - -	71
Storey, John - -	34
Storr, Dorothy - -	-25, 26
——— Joseph - -	25
——— Marmaduke - 25, 26, 47
St. Osyth - - -xiv. xxxvi.
Stubbs, John - - xxvii. 56
Stynter - - -	13
Sudbury - - -	79
Suffolk - - - liv. 5, 43
Sunderland - -	-51, 54
Surrey - xxxii. 43, 48, 56
Sussex - - -	-13, 19
Swanmore - -	-xxxii.
Swansea - - -	26
Sweden - - -	-xxxii.
Swinton, John - -	41
Sydney, Algernon - xi. 12, 29
Talantyre - - -	54
Talcot, Anna - - xliv. 76
Tauler, Johann - -	16

	PAGE
Taunton - - -	-xxxi.
Taylor, C. - - -	42
Tees - - -	liv.
Teeles, R. - - -	33
Telner, Jacob - 12, 13, 18
Tenison, Archbishop -	13
Teutschel - - -	16
Tey, Great - - -	xlvi.
Thatcher, Priest - -	56
Thaxted - - xviii. 69, 72
Thomas, Leisy - -	34
Thorncomb- - -	-xxxi.
Thorne - - -	14
——— Michael - -	71
Thurloe, Secretary -	51
Thurston, Thomas -	53
Tiler, Aunt - - -	45
Tollesbury - - -	72
Topsham - - -	-xxxi.
Torkington, Robert -	49
Totnes - - -	-xxxi.
Townsend, Simon -	-xxii.
Toyspell (or Tayspill), Giles	59
Treesmere - - -	-xxxi.
Tregonsenes - -	-xxxi.
Truro - - -	-xxxi.
Turks - - -	xxxvi.
Tuke, Samuel - -	lii.
Turner, John - -	72
——— Thomas - - xxii. xxiv.
Twisden, Judge - -	46
Two Weeks' Meeting - xxxvi. 15
Tynemouth Castle -	34
Tyrconnell, Lord -	53
Ulm - - -	17
Ulster- - -	55
Upsher, Thomas -	42
Vanderwall, John - 14, 71
——— Daniel - 49, 77
——— Mary xxv. 37, 41
Vanderwey, John - 29 (2)
Vane, Sir Harry - -	50
Van Helmont, Franciscus M.	15
Van Losevelt, Adrian -	33
Van Tongere, Bade - 15, 24
Vaughton, John - -	45
Velthusyen, Lambert van -	39
Vicars, John, Mayor - xviii. 68
Virginia - - 30, 48, 56
Wakering, Justice Dionysius	6
Wales - - - 52, 56

	PAGE
Waller, Matthew-	- - 76
—— Richard -	- 76, 77
—— Steven -	- - 76
Wallis, Elizabeth	- - xxx.
—— John	- - 15
—— Thomas -	- - 69
Walney Island -	- - 50
Waltham -	- - xviii.
Wandsworth -	- xlviii.
Warnedistel, Felis	- - 27
Wardell, Robert -	- 51, 52, 54
Warner, Sarah -	- - 44
Warsaw (Warschau) -	- 32
Warwick -	- 25, 26, 36
Warwick, Priest	- - 54
Waterlander Mennonites	- 16
Watts, Mary -	- - 76
Weatherley, George, 18, 44, 59, 60, 62, 71, 73.	
Webb, John -	- - 70
Weigel, Val. (Wegelius)	- 2
Welsh, William -	- 8, 17, 24
—— Zachary -	- - 71
Werstadt -	- - 38
Weston, William	- xxx. 29
West of England	xxx. 14, 57
West Indies	- - 52
Westmoreland -	- - xxi.
West Riding, Yorks -	14, 42
West River	- - 56
Wexford -	- - 55
Weymouth -	- - xxxi.
Whitehead, John	46, 47
—— George xlvii. xlviii. 1, 3, 8, 14. 15, 29, 45, 51, 53, 57, 64.	
Whitehaven -	- - 55

	PAGE
Wickens, William	- - 9
Wickombruck -	- - 5
Widders, Robert	- - 56
Wilkinson, John -	- 27, 34
William the Silent	- - 20
Williams, Roger -	- - 57
—— William	- - 72
Williamscote -	- - xxx.
Willis, Priest -	- - 6
Winchester -	- xxxii.
Winterbourne -	- xxx. 48
Witham -	- xviii. 6
Witmarsum -	- - 27
Wittenberg -	- - 17
Witts, Herman -	- - 79
Woerden -	- - 30
Woodbridge -	10, 11
Woolley, Ezekiel	- 17 (2)
—— Mary -	- - 17
—— William	- - 78
Worcester -	- - 4
Wormingford Lodge -	- 44
Worminghurst -	- - 42
Worms -	- xxix. 16, 38
Yarmouth -	- xxvi. 43, 60, 62
Yealand -	- - 3
Yeomans, Isabel -	- xlii. 23
Yoakley, Thomas	- - 40
York -	xxi. 14, 34, 36, 46, 47
Yorkshire xxi. xxxiii. xxxiv. xxxv. 27, 47, 50, 55.	
Zieriksee -	- - 64
Zinspenning, Judith xi. xiv. 26, 27, 59, 60.	
Zurich -	- - 28